LOVING ROWAN

WENDY SMITH

Edited by
LAUREN CLARKE

Cover Design by
BOOKISH GRAPHICS

ONE

ROWAN

NOTHING BUGGED me more than a change to my routine, and today was no exception. Right at the very last minute, my final lecture for the day had been cancelled, and I grumbled as I climbed on the bus to go home.

The house was still. Nothing unusual. With the different schedules Andrew, Charlie and I had, there weren't many times when the three of us were at home together.

"Andrew? Charlie?" I called out. *No response.* I had the house to myself.

I sat on the couch, and closed my eyes, taking a deep breath, and enjoying the quiet. Part of me wished Andrew was home. Maybe if he were, I would finally tell him how I felt.

Loud laughter came from Charlie's room, and I opened my eyes, turning my head towards the sound. A gentle click, and the door opened. There stood Andrew, his arms around Charlie's waist, his lips on hers as she laughed that throaty laugh of hers, muffled only by his kiss.

I stood, unable to take my eyes off them, watching as my two best friends made out in the doorway. Charlie's hair, loose and messy, told the story of what they'd been doing.

When he let go of her, she turned to come out the door. Our eyes locked, and her jaw dropped at the sight of me. Tears rolled down my cheeks at the sight of the one person I had entrusted with the secret of how I felt about Andrew emerging from the bedroom with the man I loved.

"Rowan. You're home," Andrew said flatly. Stabbing pain hit my stomach at his disappointment. He didn't want me here.

"Rowan, it's not what it looks like," Charlie said. I could see the strain on her face as she struggled to hold back her own tears. Of all the people in my life, she was the one who knew just how much this would hurt me.

"Of course it is," Andrew snapped. "I told you we should have just told her. All this sneaking around, and now look."

I stared at him. Talking about me as if I wasn't there. He had been my best friend from birth, and he hadn't had the decency to tell me directly. I fisted my hands, digging my fingernails into my palms as the pain of the situation gripped me. I was lost for words; it was the only way I knew how to cope.

"I'm sorry, Rowan. I knew you wouldn't like this, so I asked Andrew to keep it secret. We never meant to hurt you, I swear. We love you." Charlie reached for my arm, and I pulled back.

I shook my head. "No."

"No what?" The pity in her eyes made my insides heat up.

I sat on the couch, flicking on the television as if they weren't there. They sat either side, talking to me as if I were a child. I shut them out, disappearing into my own little world, the world inside my head where no one could hurt me. There was just noise outside that space, white noise that I couldn't completely get rid of. When it built to the point where I could no longer ignore it, I stood.

Walking past them, I went into my room and slammed the door. Screw them both.

I BURIED my head under my pillow as their voices got louder and louder outside. Maybe I should have found joy in their arguing, but instead it just made me more miserable.

"What the hell is her problem?" Andrew asked.

"What do you think? She's been in love with you forever. Damn it, Andrew, I didn't want her to find out this way."

"It's been more than three years, Charlie. She had to find out some time, and I don't want to hide anymore."

I pulled the pillow in tight. Charlie had been the one person I had confided in when it came to Andrew. I had trusted her with the contents of my heart, and she had helped shatter it.

"Neither do I," she said, "but we should have handled this better. We should have told her."

"She'll be fine. She'll find some geeky guy and settle down happily ever after."

His disregard for my feelings cut me to the quick. Andrew had always been the one who made me feel special. I hated the way I looked, tall and skinny, no boobs to speak of, and covered in freckles. He had always seemed to see past that, and I had thought that he would be more concerned with how rejected I now felt. Apparently not.

"Andrew, don't be a dick. Rowan is amazing. I feel like such a total bitch doing this to her. I never, ever wanted to hurt her." Charlie let out a loud sob, and Andrew's voice softened at the sound.

"Neither did I. I love you guys so much. I just never wanted her in that way. It was always you, Charlie. You know it was."

The sound faded as they presumably went into one of the bedrooms and I sat up, looking at myself in the dressing room mirror. My eyes were red from crying, and I wished like crazy I could be anyone else but myself. Anywhere but here.

I opened my laptop, found some music to listen to and lay down on the bed with my headphones on. At least that would drown out any more noise.

TWO

ROWAN

BREAKFAST WAS uncomfortable the next morning. I stayed in bed for as long as I could get away with to avoid seeing them, but soon my stomach grumbled, and I had to get to the bus on time.

Charlie looked up at me as I sat, so much hope in her eyes. Maybe she thought a good night's sleep would make my feelings suddenly change.

Andrew didn't even look at me, and I wasn't about to be the one to break silence.

I threw some cereal into a bowl and wolfed it down, anxious to get out and away from the tension. Charlie watched me, barely moving. I don't think she knew what to say, and I had no idea either, so I just ate.

Standing, I grabbed my bag. "I'm moving out," I said, meeting Andrew's eye.

"You don't have to," Charlie said. I turned towards her. She had bags under her eyes, and I wondered if she'd had as much luck sleeping as I had.

"Yeah, I do."

I walked out the door and down the road to the bus. The rain was falling in big, heavy drops, and I was grateful to be able to sit on the bus for half an hour, out of the awful weather.

The bus had no one else on it. This was such a quiet route I loved that I was by myself as I tucked myself down the back as usual. A bit of music would help keep my mind off everything.

Then, he was there, standing at the front of the bus and fumbling in his pocket for change, mumbling about not having enough.

The bus driver told him to hurry up, and the guy looked around helplessly. For just a moment, our eyes locked, and I felt nothing but sympathy for him. If I'd been in that situation, I would have been mortified.

"Hey, you don't have fifty cents, do you?" he called out. He grinned, as if he didn't have a care in the world, even though the driver was about to kick him back out into the pouring rain.

"Uh, sure." I dug in to my pocket, finding the right coin, and made my way to him.

"You're a lifesaver," he said, taking it from me and winking.

I went back to my seat only to find that he'd followed, sitting in the seat in front of me.

"I really appreciate your help."

Holy shit. He wants to have a conversation.

I smiled, sucking my lower lip between my teeth, trying to work out how to form words. He cocked his head, waiting for a response, and smiling a simply gorgeous smile.

"It's no problem. I think we all have those kinds of days," I mumbled.

"My car broke down. I didn't expect to have to catch a bus."

He kept smiling at me as I nodded, taking a book out of my bag to read.

"So, uh, do you catch this bus often?"

I raised an eyebrow. "Nearly every day."

"That must have sounded like a horrendous pick-up line. I didn't mean it to." He laughed, and I couldn't help smiling back, the heat in my cheeks growing as I blushed.

"I'm going to the UK tomorrow. Spending a few months travelling around Europe. Have you ever been anywhere like that?"

I shook my head. "Nope. Never been out of the country."

"Do you want to travel?"

"I haven't really thought about it."

"Neither had I. I just broke up with my girlfriend, and I'm over this place."

I exhaled loudly. "I completely get that."

Looking back at my book, I read the same chapter three times before giving up and placing it back in my bag.

When we got to my stop, he looked up as I stood, smiling at me.

"It was nice meeting you, and thanks again," he said, waving.

I nodded, swiping my bus card and stepping out onto the footpath. Turning, I caught a glimpse of him as I set off towards the university. He smiled and waved again, and for just a moment I wished I'd stayed on the bus.

Don't be silly; he's just being nice.

Being a grown-up was so hard.

THREE

ROWAN

AS I PACKED up my room, memories of moments with Charlie came to the surface. All these years she'd been the one girl I could trust. She knew what it was liked to be teased for having a boys' name, even if she was really Charlotte.

She knew what it was like to feel like an outcast. Where my sore point was my freckles, hers had been her ill health. She'd never been able to come home with me to the orchard, for fear that something in the air would set off her asthma, but everywhere else we went, we were inseparable.

I jumped as she knocked on the door. "Can we talk?"

"I'm busy."

She moved across the room, sitting on the bed. "Can't we work this out, Rowan? I know we've been stupid, but it's not worth losing our friendship over."

I squeezed the shirt I held in my hands as I looked at her. "I wish you'd been honest with me. All this time I trusted you, loved you, and you couldn't even tell me."

She looked up at me, her big, blue eyes filled with tears. "I'm sorry. I just didn't know how to tell you. Please don't leave."

I placed the shirt in the suitcase, picking up the next one. "I have to. I can't stay here and watch you two together. I could have dealt with anyone but you, Charlie. You knew how much I loved him. Now I'm the odd one out."

"We've all had turns at that, Rowan. Remember when we used to play Dad's old records? What was that Kiss song? 'I Was Made For Loving You'?" Andrew always sat to the side while we had all the fun.

I remembered. Charlie and I would play it over and over again, miming and dancing while Andrew rolled his eyes at us.

"I remember. But we were kids then; things have changed. Back then, we never would have kept any secrets from each other. Not anymore."

Charlie looked at the floor as I threw the last of my things in the bag, and carried it out to the living room.

Andrew sat on the couch, glancing up at me before looking back at the television. In all the years I'd known them, I'd never felt so much the outsider.

I dumped my house keys on the table, walking out to the car and placing my bag in the only spot left. The car was so full of all my things.

It would have been easy to go home to the orchard; Mum and Dad would welcome me with open arms. They always did. I loved that place so much. My entire childhood had been one of running through the trees, playing hide and seek with my elder sisters, Michelle and Lindsay. And Andrew. It always came back to him.

When he'd started dating, I'd tried to get over him, find someone else who would love me. The closest I came was finding someone who worked on the orchard, David. I thought he'd cared about me, but all he'd wanted was to bang the boss's daughter. Thankfully, I'd found out before that happened.

Now I was alone, and moving out by my choice, but I couldn't see any other way. It wasn't really even that they were together, it was that they'd kept it from me. We'd always been so honest with one another; the only secret I'd ever kept was my love for Andrew, and Charlie knew about that.

I drove to the student hostel near Auckland university. This would do for the last few months of the year. At least I would have a bed and a roof over my head, and not have to deal with either Andrew or Charlie.

The less I had to do with them, the better.

FOUR

KYLE

Six months later

COMING BACK to work after six months away felt great. I had a great affection for the place, and the staff. Some of them had known me since I was a kid, and this was like a second home.

I'd missed Dad at breakfast, and he was already in the office when I walked in.

"Ready for your first day back?" he asked.

"I really am. I actually missed this place."

He grinned. "Come on then, there's a few new staff, let's go for a walk."

Nothing had changed that much, until we got to the small office at the end of the building. Crouched behind the desk, plugging something in to the computer was the most beautiful shaped rear end I'd ever seen, squeezed into a pair of jeans. Perfection in denim.

"Rowan?" Dad said.

Shit. It was a guy?

She stood up, turning towards me, and I caught my breath at what I saw. I never forgot a face: it was the girl from the bus.

She had long, light brown hair, the hazel eyes I remembered from our previous encounter. And those freckles. Not just a few on her nose, but everywhere. She was like one of those models you see, the ones that stand out because they look just that little bit different. Absolutely gorgeous.

Back then I'd fallen into insta-lust, but the timing was all wrong. I'd been in recovery mode after my ex had literally thrown everything I owned out onto the lawn in the pouring rain. After all this time, I wondered if she remembered me. I saw a flash of recognition in her eyes. Had I made an impact on her too?

"Mr Warner?" She blushed, looking down at the computer.

Dad smiled. "Rowan, this is my son, Kyle. He's been travelling overseas the last six months, and has come back to head up the marketing team." He turned to me. "This is Rowan Taylor, she's our database administrator."

I held my hand out to shake hers, and she smiled as she took it. Her hand was warm, and her lips were slightly raised at the corners as she looked down shyly.

There was a row of freckles across her top lip, and my mind went blank at the sight of them.

Dad turned back towards the door, and I followed, smiling and waving at her. She was obviously very shy, but maybe I could convince her to come out of her shell, find out more about her.

She was in the staff room at lunch time, sitting apart from the other women. They all laughed and joked, but not her. She sat in the corner, eating her lunch in silence. I watched her for a moment. She was clearly the outsider.

Ignoring the chatter from the other table, I sat at the same table as Rowan, smiling as I unwrapped my sandwich. "First day back, and I think I have the most boring lunch ever." I laughed.

She shrugged. "No more boring than mine. I think I have something similar."

I took a peek over the edge of her lunchbox. "I don't know. That salad looks nice and healthy."

I grinned, and she shook her head, smiling at the table as she looked away shyly again. That was so insanely hot. She hated the attention, that much was clear, and I loved the reaction I was getting. *Do I mention the bus?*

She excused herself when she was finished, and I watched her leave, thinking about what my next move was. There was no ring, so a good chance she wasn't married. Surely she had a boyfriend.

"Don't even think about it." My father's personal assistant, Miriam, sat at the table.

"Who, me?" I grinned at her.

"She's as shy as they come. I think you would scare the crap out of her if you paid her any more attention." Miriam said, sternly.

"But is she single?"

She laughed. "I think so, but you steer clear of her. She's doing a lot of important work getting us moved onto this new computer system, and your father will be pissed at you if you scare her off."

"You know me, Miriam." I leaned across the table so the other staff couldn't hear. "I promise I'll be gentle." I winked at her and she laughed even harder.

"You wouldn't know how. Go back to work and leave the poor girl alone."

FIVE

ROWAN

I WAS CROUCHED, plugging a drive in when they walked into my office. As soon as I laid eyes on him, I knew Kyle Warner was that cute guy from the bus. All I really remembered from that day was that he talked to me as if he were really interested in what I had to say. I was still all over the place after discovering Andrew and Charlie were together. Afterwards, I'd spent hours analysing the conversation, as I was prone to do. I just didn't get other people, and trusting anyone was difficult. Even talking was difficult at times, and I practically whispered when I got shy.

He had dark hair, blue eyes, and the height I remembered. More often than not I'm as tall, if not taller than the men I meet. Not him.

Then, there was that smile. I felt so self-conscious as he'd looked me over, but I knew there was nothing to get excited about. There were plenty of girls in the office much better looking than me. When he left, I went back to my work and managed to push through a whole bunch of little issues I'd been having. The morning was really productive, it was always nice to solve a problem without any help, and I was quite proud of what I had done.

Taking out my lunch, I pulled a face. It was boring and not that appetising, but since I had moved into my apartment ever dollar counted, and I was saving as much as possible. Reluctantly, I made my way to the staff room.

The other staff were all chatting, and I always felt awkward around them. They had known each other for so long, and knew everything about each other. I was still the new girl.

I sat off to the side by myself at a small table. They all glanced at me as I sat and smiled back at them before sitting. It was a fleeting moment before they were back to their chatter, and I focused on my food, not even realising at first that he was there.

He just sat at my table, and starting talking. I was so shell-shocked he was talking to me, I can't even remember what he said, but I wanted to crawl into a hole in the ground. All I recall is him looking at my lunch for some reason, and saying it looked healthy.

What I really wanted was a cheeseburger and fries.

I looked away; his face was so animated. Did he really want to talk to me? Was he just teasing? If I left the room, would he be laughing at me too? I wish I wasn't so paranoid.

Making friends as an adult was even more difficult now than it had been when I was a child. I slunk away back to my office, where I could look online for something I'd been saving for. I'd promised myself when I had enough sitting in the bank, I would buy myself a console to play games. Most nights I curled up in bed with a laptop and streamed television shows off the net, or buried myself in a book. At least a console would give me something new to do.

Ignoring the nagging feeling in the back of my head that I should be getting out more, and meeting new people, I found the best deal and clicked buy. The feeling was exhilarating, having not bought anything nice and expensive for myself. As I filled in the credit card details, I thought of Andrew and Charlie. We'd talked about doing something like this for the house we shared, but none of us ever had the money to do it.

That thought made me feel more lonely than ever. I looked up, watching people walk up and down the corridor past my office, wishing it was easier to just put myself out there to make friends.

Instead, I went back to the website and started looking at more games that I could buy to play. The console came with a couple that were multiplayer, but also single player. I didn't need much more than that.

I clapped in excitement at the screen. With any luck it would be with me in the next few days, and I could bury myself in a world where I felt good about myself. Not this horrible real world, where I was never sure of people's intentions and too shy to approach anyone.

Without a doubt this was just another way to bury myself, and I knew it was a bad move, driving me further into my self-imposed isolation.

At the end of the day, I walked out to my car, taking a glimpse at the reception desk as I went past, just in case my package had already arrived. I knew there wasn't much chance of that, but it was worth a look.

I heard laughter as I unlocked my door, and I looked up to see Kyle Warner chatting with one of the sales reps. She was twirling her hair through her fingers, and gently rocking from side to side. As difficult as I found it to read what men were thinking, her thoughts were really out there for the world to see. She would have done him in a heartbeat.

He looked towards me, and for a moment our eyes locked. He smiled, rolling his eyes as if sharing some private joke with me that he didn't want to listen to her.

I grinned, looking down into my car, and sliding into the front seat. If I didn't know better, I'd think he was flirting, but a sinking feeling in my stomach brought me back to earth thinking of the last person who'd made me feel that way.

Closing my eyes, I sat for a moment, wondering what was behind that smile. I was probably reading too much into it. It wouldn't be the first time, and I wasn't about to lose everything because of it.

No matter how gorgeous he was.

SIX

KYLE

SHE WAS GORGEOUS; the shy looks, the almost whispered sentences when I managed to get words out of her ... For whatever reason, I wanted to wrap her in cotton wool and protect her. I imagined her to be this fragile thing that would break at the first sign of trouble.

Tall and thin, she looked awkward in her own body, but that smile, that amazing smile made the day brighter. Suffice to say, that I was very interested in Miss Rowan Taylor.

Then, she'd be asked about her project, the work she was doing for this system migration, whatever that meant. She'd light up like a child at Christmas, speaking in acronyms. I had no idea what she meant most of the time, but her soft voice was hypnotic, and I found myself paying close attention to what she was saying. Even if I didn't understand it.

Dad was clearly taken with her too, deferring to her for information instead of her manager. I suspected that was due to the old guy being due for retirement. If Rowan stuck around, she'd be the future of the company, just as I was, and I looked forward to working with her for a long time to come.

A few days after my return, I saw a courier come in with a package for her, and I jumped in to sign for it.

"I'll call Rowan and let her know it's here. I know she's been waiting for it; she's only been asking every five minutes if it's arrived," Miriam said.

"Don't worry about it. I'll swing by and drop it off." I smiled at her, and she laughed.

"Watch yourself, Kyle. Don't you upset that girl."

"Anyone would think I was a menace." I winked. She laughed, shooing me away with the package.

I strolled down the corridor, whistling as I went and waving to the staff, most of whom looked at me and shook their heads at my enthusiasm.

Dad had an unwritten rule about staff relationships, and Rowan tempted me to break it. Maybe I'd ask her out.

I turned the final corner to her office, and tapped on the door before opening it. She had bits of computer strewn all over the lino, and I shook my head, grinning at the mess.

"This arrived for you," I said, waving it around.

She raised her eyes, smiling at the sight of what was in my arms. "Can you just leave it there, by the door? I had to pull this server apart, to work out what had died. Sorry for the mess."

I shrugged. "You're just doing your job." I grinned at her, deciding to chance it and deliver it in to her arms. Gingerly, I made my way towards her before tripping over a power cord and dropping her parcel. It fell to the floor, landing with a loud crack.

"Oh, shit." I bent to pick it up.

Her jaw dropped, looking at the box. She closed her eyes briefly before holding her hands out for it.

"Rowan, if it's broken, I'll get you a new one. Whatever it is."

She shook her head. "It was my fault. Don't worry about it."

"It wasn't your fault. I should have just left it at the door."

"Don't worry about it, Kyle," she snapped, pulling the box away from me and sitting it on the bin.

"Aren't you going to open it?"

"I think that cracking sound was pretty definitive, don't you?"

She looked away, her cheeks aflame. Her reaction made me feel even more guilty.

"I need to get on with this. Thanks for bringing me the parcel," she mumbled.

"You're welcome." I scratched my head. "I guess."

Closing the door as I left, I kicked the wall on the other side of the hall. "Stupid. So Stupid."

I waited until I saw her leave for the day. Her shoulders were slumped, and there was no smile on her face as there usually was. We'd only known each other a few days, but I'd not seen her upset. She just looked miserable now.

Going into her office, I retrieved the package from where it sat on top of the bin. It was apparent that she'd opened it. The paper it was wrapped on had been ripped from the box, and the end of the box torn open. It was a gaming console, and I could see the big crack that ran down the centre of it, rendering it useless.

"Oh, crap." I could see why she was upset. She'd been waiting for it and I had screwed up, being so keen to impress her, or something. Hell, I didn't even know why I was acting like I was. Why on earth didn't I listen to her? No wonder she was pissed.

Sighing, I turned it over in my hands. I'd have to find some way to make it up to her.

SEVEN

ROWAN

I HATE BEING SO MEEK, so bad at standing up for myself. That whole incident this afternoon had upset me more than I could ever let Kyle see.

Sometimes, I wanted to break out of myself, be this laughing, smiling extrovert who could enchant others. There was a salesperson at work in particular I thought of when that thought crossed my mind. She was the one I saw in the car park flirting with Kyle. I wanted to be more like her.

I sat on the couch, fidgeting, and looking at the remains of my purchase on the coffee table. I'd rescued the controller that came with the console, and the games that were in the package. As upset as I was, I wasn't about to harass the boss's son into buying me something new.

I lay down, looking up at the ceiling, and wondering what Charlie and Andrew were doing. It was nights like this I thought of them the most, as I still tried to fill the gap. At first, I'd immersed myself in work and research that my big project required. As time progressed, the need for that had lessened, and this had been the next thing I'd thought of to take my mind off things.

Maybe I should just get a pet.

I jumped as a thud came from the door, as if something fell against it. When it happened again, I went over to the door and slowly opened it. There, large as life, was Kyle Warner, his arms full of packages and a grin across his face like the cat that got the cream.

"So, I guess the address you gave HR was right. Can I come in? This is a bit awkward."

I stood back, staring as he walked past, placing the packages on the couch. He began to unpack everything, and I raised an eyebrow at a console being pulled out of a bag, the same as the one that had broken.

"What are you doing?"

"Unpacking your new purchase."

I shook my head. "No, the one I bought broke."

"It was my fault. So, I'm righting the wrong, and replacing it."

Sighing, I closed the door, taking a step closer to the couch.

"You didn't have to do that. It was my fault the floor was a mess."

He looked up at me, his blue eyes twinkling with excitement. "Well it's too late for that, I've done it. Come on, don't you want to get this all connected?"

I chewed my bottom lip before sighing again, and rolling my eyes. "I suppose so."

Oh God, I think I'm acting like I'm about twelve.

"You can't tell me you're not just a little excited, Rowan."

Now I sucked my upper lip in, shaking my head slowly, and trying not to smile.

"Fine." I grinned, and he held his hand out for mine.

I rolled my eyes again, taking his hand as he pulled me down onto the floor beside him. "I think you need to plug all this stuff into the television. I have no idea."

Laughing, I shook my head as I crawled around the back of the TV with the cables, running them back through the cabinet to the front where the console was supposed to sit.

Working together we plugged it all in, and he sat, looking puzzled at the one controller he'd pulled out of the box. I was about to tell him that I'd rescued the one from the other box, when he reached into a bag and pulled another one out.

"I even bought one of these for me. I thought I could play with you ... I mean, we could play with each other. Damn it. I mean we could play together." He grinned, and I knew damn well his play on words had been deliberate.

I cocked an eyebrow. "Just for you?"

"Yeah. I bought a controller just for me. Is that okay?"

Sitting on the couch, I picked up a game that he'd bought. "I guess so."

"Car racing then, from the looks of what you've picked up. Hope you're a good driver. Hey, have you had dinner yet?"

It took me a moment to take in what he was saying, he spoke so quickly.

"Um, no, I hadn't thought about it."

"Let's order pizza, and we'll get started. Want to make a bet on who is going to kick who's arse?"

I just laughed, slapping my forehead. "Remind me how you came to be at my place?"

"I felt guilty. I was trying to do you a favour and bring you that package. I should have done what you asked. This is my way of apologising. Though, I have just realised that I've crashed your Friday night and not even considered that you might have a date." We locked gazes, and my heart thumped at that gorgeous smile of his.

I'm such an idiot. He's just being nice because of what happened.

"No, no date. Just a quiet night in."

"Cool. I'll order a pizza to be delivered. Anything in particular you want?"

I shook my head, watching as he dialled and ordered. This was the nicest anyone had really been to me since I'd broken up with my former best friends. Maybe I'd found a new friend. He hadn't been back in the country for long.

But deep down I knew that some day he'd find a girl as gorgeous as him, and our friendship would be shoved aside.

For now, I smiled, picked up a controller and laughed as I beat him in our first race. At least tonight would be fun. I just wish it didn't feel like he was flirting with me.

He couldn't be, could he?

EIGHT

KYLE

SHE WAS WEIRD.

I don't mean in a horrifying, running-away-from-her kind of way, but she was even more introverted than I'd thought. She was beautiful, and funny when she showed that side of herself, but she could barely talk to me without blushing. She'd go from being serious and concentrating on the game at hand, to laughing and teasing me for not being as good as her.

By the time I left her place, I was harder than I had any right to be, more aroused than I had been in a long time.

I had hoped my apology gift might make it easier to ask her out. Instead, I realised that I'd have to take things very slowly. I didn't know how much experience she had, but I doubted it was much. Not when accidentally brushing my hand against hers resulted in her pulling back, retracting like a snail into its shell. There was definitely some type of spark between us; I hoped she felt it too.

I didn't know her well enough to ask her what this was all about, whether she was just naturally shy or if something had happened to make her this way, and yet, it made me feel fiercely protective of her, as if she brought out some alpha male side of me. I had an overwhelming urge to wrap her up in my arms and growl at anyone who went near her. It was crazy and irrational, and I loved the way I felt.

For whatever reason, the feelings that were growing for her just made me happy. I wanted more, but this was the opposite of the crazy I'd lived with before. My last relationship got too serious too fast, and although this wasn't quite what I had thought would happen, I could live with taking things slow. At least for a while.

We could hang out together, get to know one another, and maybe Rowan would start to come out of that shell. I could coax her out, gaining her confidence, and we could find out together if we had a future.

I drove home thinking about her. It was probably some kind of miracle that stopped me from having an accident. That continued into the house where I rounded the corner turning into the living room and bumped into Dad. While I found a place to live, he was okay with me staying here. After my big trip I had to save money to get into a place, and I'd spent a chunk of it shopping for Rowan. I'd have to start again, but at least she was happy.

"Did you not see me?" He grinned.

"Sorry, Dad. Distracted."

"What's her name?" *Shit*. He knew me too well.

"It's complicated." I sat down on the couch.

"What's complicated about it? As long as it's not like the last time, I'd be happy for you."

I looked at my feet.

"Kyle? What is it?"

"I spent the evening with Rowan."

He cocked an eyebrow. "Rowan? Rowan from work, Rowan?"

"Well, I don't know too many other girls called Rowan, Dad."

He sighed, sitting next to me. "You know how I feel about personal relationships at work."

"Yeah, but we're just friends. At least for now."

He smiled, leaning back. "She wants more, or you do?"

"I don't know. I mean, I've only just met her, but she intrigues me. She's not like anyone I've ever met before."

"You're right, there." He nodded, patting me on the shoulder. "She appears to be doing a good job. I like her."

"Does that mean you approve?"

"If you're determined to be friends, I can live with that. Not so comfortable on the something more bit."

I shrugged. "I don't even know if she's thinking that way. She's different to anyone I've been with before, but at the same time, she's just so normal. I can imagine just sitting together and enjoying each other's company without all the drama."

He smiled. "Your mother was like that. We could just sit together for hours and never say a word. Just being together was enough." He stared into the distance, a faint smile curling his lips. "Kyle, I can warn you all you like and you don't have to listen. Just be careful. Okay?"

"Okay."

"Want a coffee? I was just about to make one."

"Sounds great."

DAD WAS GRUMBLING in the morning as he tried to turn his computer on. "Kyle, can you come and look at this. It's not turning on and I need to get some work done."

I walked into his study, and pressed the on button. Nothing happened. I shrugged. "I have no idea."

"You're helpful." He picked up the phone and dialled, sighing as he got no answer. "Damn it."

"What's wrong?"

"Ross isn't answering."

I rolled my eyes. "He's not your personal helpdesk."

"He's my IT Manager. He'll be able to help me."

"I could call Rowan."

He looked at his phone. "I don't know. Ross has helped me in the past. I don't want to stand on his toes."

"Well, he should answer his phone then. Do you want to do your work?"

We stood and looked at each other for a moment.

He nodded. "If she can help, that would be great."

I fished my phone out of my pocket, and dialled the number I'd swiped from the HR records. Rowan's sleepy voice came down the line.

"Hey sleepyhead," I said brightly.

"Kyle?"

"I was wondering if you could help me. Dad, actually."

"What's up?" She yawned and I pictured her at home in whatever she wore to bed. Maybe she wore nothing.

I grinned. "His computer won't start this morning and he can't get hold of Ross. Can you take a look at it?"

"Umm sure. Want me to come over?"

"If you could. Tell us if the computer can be fixed, or if we need to replace it."

I gave her the address before hanging up, nodding at Dad.

"Done. She's on her way over."

As soon as there was a knock on the door, I leapt up and ran, to Dad's amusement. I put my finger over my lips and looked at him as I opened it.

She looked around nervously. "Hi."

"Hey, come in." I smiled at her as she walked past me and into the house.

Dad nodded. "Thanks, Rowan. Normally Ross helps me, but I can't get hold of him."

"Let's see what's going on." She smiled, and I smirked behind her back. Buried in the things she enjoyed, she revelled in her knowledge.

She sat at Dad's desk and he sat opposite, watching her intently. Pulling the computer up from the floor, she took off the side and grimaced as a cloud of dust was dislodged.

"Got a vacuum cleaner? This isn't going to help." She looked at him as if he were stupid and should have known this all along.

I watched as my father, usually the one in control, trudged off and fetched the vacuum. He looked as if he'd been slapped, and I laughed to myself as he came back and plugged it in without a word.

She cleaned it out, and within minutes came up with a verdict.

"It looks like the motherboard. Something's gone boom in here. There's a faint electrical smell; could be something that's burned out."

He stared at her as if she had said the most important words he would ever hear.

"So what do we do to fix it, Rowan?"

"I'll pull this apart and we can see if we can find a replacement. Might be hard because it's a little old, but there's a few places I know we can try."

He lit up, and I shook my head at their interaction. She was leading the way, and he was happy to follow whatever she said.

"That would be great," he said, turning to look at me and smiling. "How much will it cost?"

She shrugged. "I don't know. If it were me, I'd probably just bite the bullet and replace the computer. Might be easier and cheaper than tracking down the parts, and as long as the hard drive is okay we can transfer the data. But, whatever you want, I'll try my best." There was that smile, the shy one that made me hot. She was steering my dad in the direction that she wanted him to go, but I doubted she was deliberately trying to manipulate him. I didn't think she was that devious.

"Whatever you think. Just do what you need to do."

"Give me your credit card, Dad. We'll go and sort it." I held my hand out and he fished it out of his wallet.

"Thanks, Rowan. I appreciate you giving up your free time for this."

"It's no problem." She looked at me. "Shall we go?"

I'd go anywhere with you.

"Sure thing."

WE ENDED up in the middle of Auckland city at a store I never knew existed, full of computer parts, and I had no idea what half of them were.

"This is our best bet. They have all kinds of random things," she said as we walked in the doorway. I stood, looking around as she turned towards a shelf near us and examined what was there.

A salesman walked towards us, came past her and straight to me. "May I help you?"

"Uh, not me. Her." I pointed at Rowan. He approached her.

"Are you looking for anything in particular?"

She came out with a whole stream of words that I did not understand in the slightest, and the salesman looked slightly uncomfortable as she spoke. I wondered if she knew more than he did. Whatever it all meant, he shook his head.

"Let's just get him a new computer. We'll be here all day at this rate." I waved his credit card in the air. "Let's go shopping."

She laughed. "I'm trying to save him money."

"He can afford it. If he wasn't so tight he would have replaced it ages ago."

"Fine." She turned back to the salesman and told him what she was looking for in a new computer. I laughed as she asked him a million questions about the components. He looked harassed by the time we got to the counter and paid for it, and I was sure he was happy to see the back of us.

For her part, she looked triumphant. She'd managed to get a decent discount, and I teased her all the way home about how she needed to relax while spending someone else's money.

She shrugged. "He's my boss."

"You don't have to try so hard to impress him. He's pretty blown away by you."

I pulled into the driveway, and she looked at me with those big, soulful eyes. "Really?"

"He was running around after you in there. You did good, Rowan. Ross will be sorry he didn't answer his phone."

She looked at her feet. "Do you think he'll be annoyed?"

"Whatever. It's just sorting out Dad's home computer."

"Yeah, but he's in charge of all of that stuff. Maybe I shouldn't be treading on his toes."

I put my hand over hers. "Don't even worry about it. Dad will be really grateful for what you've done. I might even make you lunch, if you're lucky."

She nodded. "At least we got you out for some fresh air. Better than being stuck inside playing games," I said.

Rowan rolled her eyes, and opened the door. She had the back of the car up and was carrying the computer inside before I could stop her.

Dad waited inside, wringing his hands as we came in the door.

"We bought you a new computer, Dad," I said.

"Can we get everything off the other one?" he asked.

"I'll go and work on that right now." Rowan smiled.

NINE

ROWAN

ADJUSTING to Kyle being around was easy. He was so sweet and kind, and made me laugh more than anyone else ever had. We were soon spending so much time together, we might as well have been roommates.

It was weird. My whole life there had been very few people I could really relax around, but Kyle was one of them. With no competition, I had him all to myself; there was no Charlie to share. Before long, I was in love with him.

Tormented by my feelings, I kept it to myself. I was too scared to tell him just in case he only wanted my friendship. The last thing I wanted was to lose another friend. I was all too painfully aware that I was back in the same sort of situation I'd started in.

He would fall asleep on the couch while watching movies after spending the evening playing games on the console. I'd sit and watch his chest rise and fall as he breathed—he was so beautiful—and I'd chew my bottom lip, just wanting to reach out and touch him.

The thick, dark, wavy hair and long eyelashes any girl would envy made my heart flutter. But I'd been here before, and it hurt. Still, Kyle was sincere, and the more time we spent together just being friends, the more I believed that maybe one day there might be something between us.

I wasn't going to build my hopes up. Not again.

I'd cover him with a blanket, and leave him there, going to sleep in my cold bed and looking at the ceiling, feeling conflicted. Neither Kyle nor Andrew wanted anything more than my friendship. At least, that's how it seemed. Kyle hadn't made a move and I would have died before saying anything to him.

Helping his father out had helped us grow closer, but I couldn't tell him what had been bugging me for weeks: my deteriorating relationship with Ross.

He was increasingly difficult to work with, and I wondered if he viewed me as a threat. I was sure my friendship with Kyle had made things worse, and helping his father with his computer? I think that was the kiss of death as far as he was concerned.

The first test for moving data was coming up. I'd put together the new system and it was humming along nicely. Now, it just needed the data converted to the right format and for it to be moved. That was nerve-racking. If I didn't get this right first time, it would give Ross an opportunity to screw me over.

The thought of that made me feel sick and I went over the code I'd written for the data conversion a million times the night before we were due to process the first batch.

It was late when I went to sleep. The next day was do or die.

I ARRIVED in my office nice and early, and went to sit at the computer. Something wasn't right. My chair had been pulled out, and some of the papers were a bit messed up, like someone had been through them. Ignoring that nagging feeling, I sat down. Sometimes the cleaners moved things around, and while it drove me nuts, there wasn't much I could do about it.

I sighed, and flicked the screen on.

"Good morning, Rowan." Ross came in and sat down opposite me. "So today's the big day, huh?"

"Looks like it."

"You nervous?" he asked, leaning on the desk on his elbows.

"A little, but the script has been setup and is ready to run. The first batch should be done by lunchtime."

He nodded. "Well, off you go."

I took a deep breath. The data had all been backed up, but to have to recover it would be admitting failure.

Smiling, I hit the keys that would start the process. I could monitor how far through it was, but the end result would have to wait for it to finish to make sure it had worked.

The morning crawled. Kyle stuck his head in my office to see if I wanted a coffee, but I was paranoid that if I took my eyes off the screen for one minute, something would go wrong.

"You'll be fine. You spent long enough working on it," he said.

"I know, but I need to be sure."

I crossed my fingers as I watched the screen. The data was processing, and quite quickly. Soon enough my wait would be over.

Ross was back in my office when it finished, hanging around, looking over my shoulder, and it unnerved me.

I went to the new database and clicked import. The system said no with a resounding beep and an error message. The data was corrupt, useless. My entire morning waiting for this and it was completely screwed. I wanted to scream at the screen, but Ross's presence stopped me from losing control. I would not do that in front of him.

"Oh. That's no good," he said, leaning over my shoulder.

"I don't understand."

"Clearly your coding had an error in it, Rowan. You'll have to recover the backup and start again once you've found the problem."

This was going to set me back some time. I'd have to recover the data and go through testing again to find the issues. "But it was working perfectly yesterday." I looked at him to see his reaction, but he was blank. I didn't understand it.

He patted me on the back. "You'll get it right, I'm sure. I'll leave you to it."

I felt sick. As pleasant as he'd been, he still made my skin crawl when he was near me.

I went to retrieve the backup. The existing systems were ancient, still relying on tape backup, and the tape wasn't where it was meant to be. My stomach sank as I turned the room upside down looking for it. It was nowhere to be found.

I went back to my office. It must be there. I'd worry about it after I worked out what was wrong with my script.

I saw it straight away. That rogue line of coding that wasn't supposed to be there. Like everything else, I was particular about how I did things, and it stuck out like a sore thumb.

Miriam knocked on the door. "Rowan, Mr Warner wants to see you in his office."

"Okay."

"Just so you know, Ross is in his office, and neither of them look happy."

I felt the colour drain from my face, my stomach churning as I struggled with my growing anger. While this had been a run-through with real data, there had been backup procedures in place; it had all been covered.

I stood, shaking as I took a deep breath before heading out the door. It was now or never. Only one person could have done this, and I could only guess that it was Ross's reaction to my growing relationships with the Warners.

I passed Kyle's office on the way, and saw him look up out of the corner of my eye. If I stopped, I'd start crying, and I wasn't going to involve him.

Taking a deep breath, I knocked on Mr Warner's door, and he called out to me to enter the room.

He pointed at a chair, giving me a small smile. "Please sit, Rowan."

I sat and tried to meet his eyes, failing.

"I hear there's been a failure of our first cutover this morning."

Swallowing hard, I nodded. "Unfortunately things did not go to plan."

"And the backup is missing."

I looked up. How did he know that? Unless Ross had gone to look, too. The confirmation that he had framed me hit me like a hammer. I'd done all of the donkey work, and now he was going to swing in and look like the hero. His reputation beyond reproach, mine in tatters.

"Mr Warner ..."

"Rowan, you know how highly I regard you and your work. This is very disappointing, to say the least."

"But, I ..."

Ross leaned over. "I can take over the project from here if need be. Give Rowan a break."

I glared at him. "I've done all of the work. I just need to find the backup or work out how to fix the data."

"Fixing the data isn't likely. This is a real mess that you've got us into, Rowan. If I have to step in, then I will."

Mr Warner sighed. "I'm sorry, Rowan. Ross is right. This was a big project for you to take on so early, and you've done so well so far. I think Ross needs to take over from here."

"I'll need the code you wrote for the conversion. I'll find what's wrong with it and fix it going forward."

"You mean the extra bit you added to break my script?" I said the words before I thought about them.

"I don't know what you mean."

"Do you think I don't recognise my own coding versus someone else's, someone who has just slapped in some messy crap in the middle of it?"

When he glared at me, I smiled sweetly.

"Are you saying your coding was interfered with, Rowan?" asked Mr Warner.

"I went over it and over it last night to make sure it was clean for this morning. I didn't think I had to check it again this morning, but afterwards I looked to see if I could find the problem. Someone had been in and changed it."

"You're paranoid," Ross sneered.

Mr Warner closed his eyes and sighed again. He was torn; I could see that. He had no reason to disbelieve me, and no reason to disbelieve Ross. There wouldn't be a way to prove anything; Ross would have seen to that.

"Okay, well, how about Ross takes over the conversion once we find this backup. I'm sorry, Rowan. I'd like to believe what you're saying is true, because I don't think you'd lie to me. But, I don't think Ross would lie to me either, and I can't risk the rest of this cutover."

"So I have to hand over all the work I've done the last few months so Ross can finish the project?"

He nodded.

"Fine." I crossed my arms defiantly, the sides of my head throbbing as my anxiety levels rose. I had no way out of this. Either I could get hysterical and get nowhere, or I could just go with it and hope he screwed up.

"Thanks. Get it all together and you can hand it over in the morning. Take another look for that backup before you go home. If we can't find it, well, I don't know what we're going to do, but we have to try."

I nodded, unable to say anything else. This was humiliating, and I wanted to run away and never come back. I thought when I came here that they wanted me, but Ross had only wanted me to do the hard yards. He wasn't interested whether I reaped the rewards.

"You can go now, Rowan. Once the system is cut over, you'll be working on the day to day maintenance of the system. Nothing is going to change with regards to that." Mr Warner smiled a little and I nodded, standing and walking out without turning back. Closing the door behind me, I shut my eyes and took a deep breath.

"Rowan?" Kyle was sitting outside the office, concern written all over his face.

"I have to go back to my office." I knew I was pale and I felt faint. The sooner I got to a chair, the better, and I needed privacy.

"Hey." He tried to grab my arm, but I kept walking away. I couldn't do this, not now. This wasn't his problem; it was mine.

TEN

KYLE

I HAD no idea what had happened, but whatever it was it was nothing good. This whole project had reached the point where Rowan's work would be under real scrutiny, and while I didn't know what was going on, her appearance told me everything.

She rushed past my office on the way to Dad's. I only caught a glimpse of her, but she didn't look her usual pretty, happy self. I waited while she was in there, and saw just how miserable she looked when she came back out. Her skin was ashen, and the tears were forming that would no doubt fall when she got back to her office.

I tried to reach out to her, help her, but she just wanted to get out of there. Ross appeared next, grinning smugly about something, and I knew he'd been behind whatever it was. He was another person I'd known for years, and he was territorial when it came to anything to do with the computer network. It had surprised me that he'd let Dad hire someone for this, but it was such a big job, and the new system would need supporting, so it did make sense.

"Dad?" I said, standing in the doorway of his office.

He shook his head, placing it in his hands before looking back up at me.

"What happened?"

"Rowan's first attempt at the database migration failed. It didn't just fail; the data is corrupt and the back up is nowhere to be found. I could have fired her for this, Kyle. She's done so much work, and I get that it's disappointing for her, but I'm wondering if I should have employed someone so young. When confronted, she tried to blame her errors on Ross. I think she's just in over her head a bit and needed to ask for help. She had it all on paper, and was confident in her ability, but maybe that wasn't enough."

"Don't you dare."

"What?"

"Rowan didn't do this. She spent hours lining everything up for today. Somehow Ross is responsible. He's pissed that she helped you out, and he's waited until he can pick up the pieces of the project."

"Rowan thinks he had something to do with it too. But he's been with me for twenty years. Hiring her was to make things easier for him. Why would he want to sabotage her?"

"He's jealous, Dad. Plain and simple. She's younger and has so much more talent than he does."

He sat back in his chair. "Kyle, I know that you care about her ..."

"That's not even the point."

"Of course you're going to defend her, and I don't blame you. But this isn't something I can be sentimental about. This is business."

"I get that, Dad, but you need to open your eyes."

He sighed. "Maybe you do."

I turned on my heel and walked from the room, slamming the door. In the time I'd spent working for him, I'd never disrespected him in the office, but this worth fighting for. I didn't even know the truth, but I would defend her to the end. I had faith in her.

She was crying in her office when I got there, her chair turned away from the door to hide it. I walked around her desk. Her hands were covering her face.

"Hey," I said, bending down and pulling her hands away.

She wouldn't meet my eyes, but this wasn't a time for her to shy away from me. I was on her side, and I needed to make her see.

"Everything is so screwed up. Your dad will never trust me again," she said, in between short, sharp breaths.

"Tell me everything that happened."

"I checked everything last night, didn't recheck it this morning because I didn't need to. Only, there are some lines of code in my script that I did not write, and it's screwed the data. The backup tape is missing, and I have no proof of anyone else doing anything."

I raised her face with my finger under her chin. "I believe you."

She exhaled loudly, and threw her arms around my neck. "Thank you."

"Hey, I know you better than anyone here, and I know how serious you are about your work. If you say that's what happened, then that's what happened. Besides, I don't think you have it in you to lie; not really."

As she let go, our faces were inches apart, and I smoothed her hair with my hand. It would have been so easy to kiss her, but she was in no state to confuse her even further. She seemed comforted by my touch, and nodded. "This was really important to me. I swear I didn't screw up."

Ross appeared in the doorway, cocking an eyebrow. "I found the back-up tape, Rowan. Can you just email me a copy of the script, and I'll sort everything out?"

I glared at him. "How convenient."

"I have no idea what you're talking about," he said as he turned and walked away.

"Scum," I said. "He's worked for Dad for years, and this is the way he acts. On the bright side, at least you know he thinks you're good enough to threaten his position. He's had it all to himself for far too long. It was Dad's idea to get in someone to manage this, and I really think it was over his head."

"I'm glad you're on my side," whispered Rowan. After all the time we'd spent together the last few weeks, we were closer than ever.

I kissed her cheek. "Always."

ELEVEN

KYLE

I'M HER FRIEND.

I thought we were just hanging out together, and that things would take a romantic turn, and the more time we spent together, the further she crept out of that shy shell. The Ross incident had brought us closer, and when we were together, she was more alive and vibrant than before. She trusted me.

Now, she was curled up on the couch with her head in my lap, not doing what I fantasised about, but sleeping.

We had decided to watch a movie, and somehow that's how we ended up. It was a full-on action flick, but I knew it had been a long week for Rowan. Now Ross had taken control of her project, she was even more stressed about it going perfectly. There hadn't been any more incidents, but I was wary of him, and acutely aware that he could persuade Dad they didn't need Rowan after all.

It wasn't fair, and I admired her for her calm about the whole thing. After that first day, she'd held her head up proudly, determined not to let Ross interfere any further. I'd tried to talk to Dad about it again, but he had made up his mind. I understood that twenty years of friendship was stronger than his connection to a girl he barely knew.

When we weren't talking about the work situation, we got back to getting to know each other. I'd heard all about Andrew and Charlie, how heartbroken she had been by the secrets they kept. She was so shy and awkward, she didn't know how to have a romantic relationship. All this time we'd spent together, I'd hoped to guide her in that direction, but either this was happening slower than I'd thought it would, or it wasn't happening at all.

She sighed in her sleep, moving slightly, and I tentatively put my hand on her head, stroking her hair. I would have sat like this all night if I had to, if she needed me.

My insta-lust was turning into love, and I had no idea how to handle it. This woman was the most amazing that I'd ever met; beautiful, and smart. She was just perfect, and I was her friend.

Damn it.

Her hair was soft to the touch, and I let it play through my fingers. This was what I wanted; she was what I wanted. No more holding back; I had to tell her and hope for the best. When she woke, I'd make a move.

She moved under my hand, stirring and turning her head to get comfortable. "Andrew," she murmured.

The moment lost, I pulled my hand away. He had to become a thing of the past before we could have a future.

Gently, I slid out from under her, placing her head gently on the couch. Fast asleep, she nestled down into the cushions and I leaned over to kiss her cheek before I left. One last look back at the door and I left.

OF COURSE I was back the next day, sitting beside her on the couch as if nothing had happened. Getting her to forget Andrew would be the tough part, but it couldn't be impossible. Could it?

"Let's go out for dinner," I said. My hand ached from playing on the console, and I wanted a change of scenery. It wasn't good for her to be stuck inside all the time either.

"Can't we just order pizza?" She pouted, and that row of freckles above her top lip made me want to kiss her more than ever. This just wasn't fair.

"How about we go up to the mall? Sit in the food court, and order whatever we feel like. I'll buy."

She nodded. "That does sound good. There's a fried chicken place I did want to try there."

I grinned. "Now you're talking. Let's go."

There were a few people walking around, going in and out of stores as they went for an evening walk. Rowan pulled me towards the food court, chatting excitedly about getting back home to kick my butt in the game we'd been playing.

I laughed, shaking my head at her. "Addict."

"Nah, I'm just better than you." She poked her tongue out at me, and I rolled my eyes as we got to our destination.

I looked around. There were quite a lot of people scattered around the food court, but finding a table wouldn't be an issue. I felt an elbow in my ribs as Rowan nudged me.

"Ouch."

"What did you want?"

I looked up at the menu. "I don't know. What are you having?"

"The chicken and chip combo with drink." She pointed at the menu. "That one."

"Can we make that two of those?" I smiled at the girl behind the counter, pulling out my wallet to pay.

"I'll go and find a table," Rowan said. I watched as she walked away, a bounce in her step. Her enjoyment of our outing made me smile. I loved seeing her happy.

She waved at me when she sat down, and our eyes met across the food court. When she was happy, her whole face just lit up. She looked so beautiful, I wanted to kiss her again.

"Down, boy," I muttered to myself.

I made my way over to the table with the food, and she sorted it all out in the regimented way she handled everything. So much of the time, my life was haphazard, I had no order to it. Rowan's life was organised, and she broke her activities into specific slots of time. I think it was her way of coping with being alone. I had thrown her schedule into disarray.

Not sorry.

"How come you're so organised?" I said. "I'd be tempted to just throw all the food onto the tray and we help ourselves."

She looked at me, one eyebrow cocked. "I like everything to be in order. Just like my work."

"We're not at work, Rowan. We're in playtime." I dangled a fry in front of her nose, and laughed as she bit at it, grabbing the end of it and sucking it into her mouth.

"Is that right, young lady?" I asked, waggling my eyebrows at her for effect. She blushed, looking down at the table and shaking her head at me.

She picked up a fry, throwing it at my face and hitting me square on the nose. "Oh, like that, is it?" I laughed.

Her delicate laughter filled the quiet hall and I loved the sound of her enjoying herself away from work, and playing games. Out in the real world, with real people around. She was full of life, and I had never loved her more.

"Rowan, I ..." I started to say something, wanting to have a real conversation about it. After weeks of skirting around the issue, I needed to know how she felt, if she could love me in return. I hadn't been looking for love, but arrived back at just the right time to find it.

She wasn't looking at me anymore. Her eyes were focused on an approaching couple, and I realised I'd seen them somewhere before from photos she'd once shown me. This was the famous Andrew and Charlie.

He was easily as tall as I was, but blond, with chiselled features. Charlie was shorter than Rowan, curvy and voluptuous, and wearing a low-cut top that showed off her cleavage. I had to admit, they were a striking couple. I looked back at Rowan. Her lips were downturned, and she looked like she was fighting the frown that threatened to take over her face.

I grabbed her hand under the table, squeezing it in reassurance. She squeezed back before taking a deep breath and letting go.

TWELVE

ROWAN

I COULDN'T BELIEVE it when I saw them. Of all the places to run into Andrew and Charlie. All I could do was stare while Charlie smiled and waved at me. I could see her eyeing up Kyle. It made me feel fiercely protective of him. She'd already taken one friend away from me.

I glanced at Kyle, knowing exactly what he was looking at. Charlie was gorgeous, and I just knew his eyes were focused on that low-cut top she wore. Just seeing her made me feel so woefully inadequate.

Looking down at the table, I avoided their eyes as they came closer. Kyle grabbed hold of my hand and squeezed, and I squeezed back, looking up to see a broad smile on his face.

"You okay?" he whispered.

I nodded.

"So, that's them?"

I nodded again.

"Rowan." Charlie leaned over to kiss me on the cheek, and she raised an eyebrow at me.

"Charlie," I replied.

Andrew sat on the other side of the table from us. "How's it going? It's been ages."

"Yeah, it has," I said, stuffing food in my face.

Andrew looked Kyle up and down, and I felt Kyle's hand on my leg, gently squeezing my knee.

"This is Kyle," I mumbled through a mouthful of food. "Kyle, this is Andrew and Charlie."

Kyle smiled at Andrew and Charlie. "Hey."

"So, what are you doing here?" Charlie asked, sitting beside Andrew.

"Taking a break from our busy evening. We needed some fresh air," said Kyle.

Andrew nodded, locking eyes with me. I knew that look. It was the *what do you think you're doing* look. As if he had any right to ask.

"I wanted to try this place. I'd heard lots of good things about it. The food is amazing," I said, waving a chicken drumstick in the air. Anything to avoid a personal conversation.

"We should get something to eat," said Andrew, looking at Charlie. She nodded, and he got up to walk to the food stand, nodding at her to follow.

"I think we should eat up and get out of here," said Kyle. "Unless you want to hang out with them."

"I thought you might like to stay and look at Charlie some more," I said, smiling sweetly.

"What makes you think that? I've never been into blondes. I'd much rather hang out with you. Besides, didn't you promise to kick my butt?"

I laughed, despite knowing he had been eyeing up Charlie. Everyone did.

"You know it. I don't particularly want to hang out with them, either. I'd much rather be at home." He gave me this look that made my heart skip a beat. If I was the type of woman to talk that way, I would totally admit to being hot for him.

He just wants to be friends, Rowan. You have to stop thinking of him that way.

"Eat quickly then, and let's get out of here. It's warmer at your place too, and your couch is so much more comfortable than these chairs."

WE DIDN'T STOP to say goodbye to Andrew and Charlie, and I pictured them returning to the table and finding it empty. I didn't care.

Kyle wanted to spend time with me, and every day I fell a little bit deeper.He reassured me, protected me, cared about me.

I was in over my head again, and I didn't care. Every moment we spent together meant so much. It even took my mind off all the crap at work.

It would have been easy to hold what was happening against Kyle, but he was so supportive and believed in me. In that regard, he'd been a much better friend than Andrew or Charlie. They were welcome to each other.

The realisation of that overwhelmed me, and I yelped as I realised that I had moved on. It was time to stop dwelling on those two.

"Are you okay?" Kyle asked. We were in the car going back to my place, and he looked at me, his brows furrowed in concern as we sat at the traffic lights waiting for them to turn green.

"Better than I have been in a long time." I couldn't stop grinning. Even if we were only destined to be friends, I felt more free of the past than ever.

THIRTEEN

KYLE

MAYBE TONIGHT WOULD BE the night to tell her how I felt. We were so close, and although I knew she occasionally saw them in passing, Andrew and Charlie were a thing of the past.

I stopped along the way at a florist to buy some roses. Something romantic for my girl to show her how much I cared.

I love you, Rowan.

Just thinking the words made me smile. She already had my heart, now I wanted to give her the rest. I wanted to bury myself so deep inside her that she would forget Andrew Carmichael ever existed.

There was nothing I wanted more than to touch her, taste her, show her how much I wanted her. Not just sexually, but in everything.

My quiet girl, who started off so shy with me, once we got to know each other better showed that her confidence had bloomed, and now she shared more and more.

If I got this right, maybe we could share for the rest of our lives. But I had to get tonight out of the way first. I'd always considered myself very self-confident. Now, I had butterflies as I thought of saying the words I was thinking.

This was crazy. No woman had ever affected me this way. Rowan was so sweet and gentle, so kind and sexy. She was simply perfect.

I shook my head at my thoughts, laughing out loud as some soppy song came on the radio. It had been a long time since I'd felt anything resembling love, and my thoughts didn't even sound like my own.

Pulling up outside the building, I gathered the roses to carry into the building. It was corny, but Rowan liked corny. We'd spent hours watching awful B-grade movies, searching the internet for the ones with the lowest ratings. Some of them had been horrendous, but we'd laughed until our sides ached.

I knocked on the door, still trying to work out how to hold the flowers to present to her. A sharp pain in my thumb told me I'd found a thorn, and she opened the door to me sucking on my thumb to stop the bleeding. How romantic.

Her eyes were red and swollen from crying, and she flew into my arms as the door opened, not even noticing the roses.

"Hey, what's going on?" I asked her pushing her back to look at her face. A crimson spot slowly spread on her shoulder where my thumb landed. "Shit, sorry. I caught my thumb on a thorn."

She frowned, her eyes dazed as she took me in. "You bought me flowers?"

"Yeah. Uh, can we go inside, and not stand in the doorway?"

"Sure," she said, taking a step back. There were tissues all over the couch. She must have been crying for hours. I looked around for somewhere to put the roses.

"Just put them on the coffee table. How did you know I needed cheering up?"

"I don't know. Just call it intuition." What I had in mind could wait. Something was up and I needed to find out what it was to work out how to fix it. "What's wrong, Rowan?"

She started picking up tissues, gathering them in her hands to throw in the bin. Every few seconds she'd sniff, holding back whatever it was that caused her to cry in the first place. I sat on the couch, staring at the flowers. So much for my big declaration of love.

Returning to the room, she sat beside me, her head on my shoulder, her chest rising and falling in sharp, short breaths. "Are you going to tell me what's wrong?"

"Charlie called me."

Oh dear God, not them again.

"And?"

"They're getting married. Soon. Must have been planning it for a while."

That explained the tears. Andrew would be completely out of reach. All the better for me. Maybe she would finally open her eyes to the world around her, instead of this relentless tunnel vision she had where he was concerned.

"Well, I guess it was kind of inevitable. That's what people do when they're in love."

"I guess. I just always thought it would be me." Her voice had dropped to a whisper.

I sighed, slipping my arm around her shoulder. "I know. But it's time to move on with your life now. There's a whole world out there."

She raised her head, looking at me through tear-filled eyes. "What would I do without you? I'm so glad you're my friend. I don't know how I would get through things like this by myself."

"You never have to worry about that, sweetheart. I'll be here whenever you need me."

Her face was inches from mine, but I resisted the temptation again to kiss her. This could go either way, and I didn't want to do anything that might cause her to keep her distance.

"Will you come to the wedding with me?"

I swallowed down the wave of nausea that swept over me. If her behaviour now was any indication, she'd be inconsolable when they were married.

"Of course. I will do whatever you want."

So much meaning behind the words, more than she realised. She smiled the faintest of smiles, and I kissed her nose affectionately. "I'll always be here for you, Rowan. No matter what happens."

"Until you meet someone and fall in love."

I pulled her into my chest, closing my eyes as I kissed the top of her head. "I don't know about that. I'm happy being right here with you."

"That's because you're a true friend. I'm sorry if I ever doubted you."

"You never have anything to feel sorry about."

We sat as I held her until her breathing returned to normal and she finally let go, smiling a tiny smile at me.

"Thanks, Kyle."

"Any time, sweetheart."

Shit. Now is not the time to screw with her head.

Our gazes locked, and I was lost in the warmth I found. Despite her upset, her eyes told the story that I always wanted to see. She did have feelings for me.

"Rowan," I whispered.

She lunged forward, brushing my lips with hers before withdrawing just as quickly.

"Rowan?"

She pulled away from me, scooting down to the other end of the couch.

"I'm sorry," she whispered.

"I told you. You never have anything to feel sorry about."

"Can we just watch a movie or something? I want to take my mind off everything."

I moved closer. "Don't you want to talk about what just happened?"

"I'm tired from crying, and I can't think straight."

She closed her eyes, and I sighed. "Fine. What do you want to watch?"

"You choose. I don't care."

I plucked one of her favourite movies from the DVD case and put it into the player. Sitting back down, I picked up the remote control, and felt her touch my arm.

She smiled. "Thank you for understanding."

"How about I go and make some hot chocolate? That'll make you feel better."

"I'd like that."

I went to the kitchen and stood staring at the wall as I waited for the water to boil. Everything was such a mess, and I had no idea what to do. How could she still be so tied up in their world that she was so affected by this? I had hoped that together we were moving on, even if we weren't a couple.

She had been wounded so deeply, more than I'd thought. They were moving on without her, which was to be expected, but the news of Andrew and Charlie's engagement had hurt her in a way I couldn't imagine.

You have to stick it out and be there for her.

I carried the cups back out to the living room and found her fast asleep, her head resting on the arm of the couch.

Smiling, I put the cups on the coffee table, and grabbed the blanket that she joked belonged to me, she'd covered me with it enough times when I'd fallen asleep. Gently, I placed it over her. She must have been exhausted from crying. I kissed her on the forehead, and left, closing the door quietly behind me.

"We'll get this wedding out of the way, and those two can go to hell," I muttered.

FOURTEEN

KYLE

I WAS ALMOST LOOKING FORWARD to the wedding. Once it was over and done with, I could be there to take care of Rowan. I was sure that she had moved on anyway, but it didn't surprise me that she was hurting.

Charlie had reappeared in her life, making overtures towards her to renew their friendship while she planned the wedding. Rowan was cautious, but soon got lost in the world of bridal magazines. It was good for her to have friends, but I knew she'd been hurt by them in the past. I didn't resent her having another companion; I was annoyed at who it was.

I'd broached the subject of the kiss several times the past month, but Rowan had been so pre-occupied with this damn wedding that she hadn't wanted to talk about it.

While they talked weddings, our evenings together all but disappeared, but Rowan was always happy to see me and would hug me hello as if nothing had happened. As far as I was concerned, that wedding couldn't come soon enough.

I guess it distracted her from work as well. Ross had gone from trying to undermine her to being downright unpleasant. Everything she touched was scrutinised by him and I knew she felt the pressure of being watched. For someone who was so sure of her skills, and rightfully so, it was a difficult situation. Dad knew how I felt, but he felt confident his man in charge would take care of things.

It was time to move out and find a place of my own. Without Rowan around, I got to looking for my own apartment, and found a nice one not too far from her. I couldn't help it; I needed to be near in case she needed me when it all fell apart.

She turned up in my office a week before the wedding, watching me from the door while I worked, and it took a few minutes for me to realise she was there.

"Hey," she said, "long time no see."

"That's not my fault."

"I've been a bad friend, and I'm sorry. I wondered if you were still up for going away with me this coming weekend?"

I nodded. "You know I am. Any time you need me, I'll be there." She smiled shyly at me, and my stomach flipped as our eyes met. It didn't matter that we hadn't spent time together these past few weeks, the magic was still there.

"Great. The wedding's on Saturday, so I wondered if you wanted to take Friday off and stay two nights, come back Sunday."

"Sounds good."

"I thought we could drive down so I can show you the sights along the way. You can stay with me at Mum and Dad's place."

I grinned, knowing how close she was to her parents. Getting on their good side would mean a lot if I wanted to get serious with her. Besides, I wanted to see this famous orchard that she'd described in such a way that I could almost see it. It was clear she loved it, and I was envious, having grown up in the city. We'd had a garden, but nothing like she'd had to play in. I would have given anything to have had a childhood like she described; instead, I'd dealt with Mum's health declining and Dad barely coping.

When she'd died, my presence had been the only thing that had kept Dad sane. I hated that I now felt further away from him than ever, thanks to this whole Ross thing.

"I'll come and pick you up on Friday morning," I said, "I'm living not far from you now."

"You moved out from your father's place? When did that happen? I feel awful that I didn't know."

"I couldn't stay there. We aren't that close right now."

She came in, sitting on the seat opposite. "Is it because of me?"

"Rowan, don't."

"It is, then. This whole mess has caused trouble between you and your father. That's the last thing I wanted."

I sat back in the chair and looked at the ceiling. "I have faith in you. He needs to understand that, and he needs to admit that he could be wrong."

When I looked back at her, she was frowning. "I never wanted to come between you and your father, Kyle."

I shrugged. "We can't agree on everything. He'll come around. He has to." I got up and walked around the desk, sitting between it and her. "I don't plan on not having you in my life any time soon."

She smiled. "I'm glad. I kind of like you being around too."

"Maybe we can talk about that some more this weekend."

"Maybe."

This had to be the closest we had gotten to actual flirting in a long time. We gazed at each other.

"Right," she said, "I have work to do, and Ross is all over every-thing, so if I'm going to take Friday off I need to get moving."

She stood and turned towards the door.

"Rowan?"

"Yes?" She looked back over her shoulder.

"I'm looking forward to spending some time together. It's been a while."

She smiled and nodded, closing the door quietly behind her as she left.

FRIDAY WAS SUNNY, with a cool gentle breeze that flowed through the open windows of the car, keeping the temperature comfortable. Perfect driving weather.

We'd tossed a coin over who was behind the wheel. Rowan was capable, but got nervous on busy roads, and I think the pressure of driving long distance with me was a bit much for her.

She'd done the trip multiple times by herself, but for some reason, she was convinced I would be one of those really annoying backseat drivers. Besides, we'd decided to take my car; it was bigger, and she could fit all the random things she'd decided to take to her parents' home with her.

Losing the coin toss, I climbed into the driver's seat, grumbling as I did.

Rowan laughed. "You'll be fine, you big baby."

"I don't really mind. It's better than risking you driving my car."

She leaned over and pinched my ear lobe. "Ouch," I said. "Cheeky wench."

Cocking an eyebrow, she grinned. "What did you call me?"

"Nothing."

She laughed, reaching into her bag for her sunglasses, and settling back into the seat.

"Comfortable?" I asked.

"Very. These seats are so much better than the seats in my car. They'll be great for sleeping in."

I pouted. "So you'll sleep while I drive all by my lonesome?"

Rowan nodded. "It's inevitable. I'm a hopeless passenger. I always fall asleep on long trips."

"I hope you don't fall asleep when you're driving." I grinned.

"Nope. But, now that's what I have you for. To drive while I sleep."

Laughing, I started the car, pulling into the traffic. "Glad I'm good for something."

As we pulled up to a red light, I felt a hand on my arm. She'd removed her sunglasses and frowned at me. "I didn't just ask you to this so you could drive. It means a lot that you're with me."

My sweet Rowan, always taking things so seriously. I smiled. "I know, sweetheart. I'm not really upset. Though I feel like haven't seen you in weeks."

She rolled her eyes, leaning back in her seat. "I'm sorry. Charlie just kept asking for my help, and wanted to mend some fences, so I decided, given that I've moved on to help her out. It doesn't mean we're best friends again. She spent ages looking at bridesmaid dresses. You should see the wedding dress, though; she's going to be a beautiful bride. I don't think I'll see much of her after the wedding, though."

The light went green, and we began to move. Once we got out of the city, the traffic would lessen and we would be able to enjoy the drive.

"Why not?" I asked, confused. Not that I would complain. The less time she spent with Charlie, the more time she'd have for me.

"They'll be newlyweds. They're not going to want me hanging around."

I glanced at her. She chewed on her bottom lip while looking out the window. "Anything else?" I asked, just knowing there had to be something more she didn't want to say.

"I missed you," she said, barely above a whisper. The words didn't have to be loud for me to love how they felt.

SHE FELL asleep at around the halfway mark, just after we'd stopped and had lunch. The road was smooth, without much traffic, and we got a clear ride all the way through to her parents' place. I didn't bother waking her; the GPS found the way easily, and I saw her orchard for the first time.

The house sat in the middle of the property, tall and majestic, rising above the apple trees. It was one of those big old farmhouses you see in the movies. A veranda ran all the way around the outside, and from the swing-seat and assorted chairs, it was clearly a family home.

An older man sat on the steps, standing as I drove into the yard. I guessed it was Rowan's dad, waiting for her to arrive.

Pulling up beside the other parked cars, I got out, and walked around the car to open Rowan's door. Her father got there as I did, extending his hand for me to shake. I grinned, taking his hand in mine. His grip was firm as he looked me up and down.

"Guess you must be Kyle," he said, grinning.

"You must be Rowan's father," I replied.

"That's me. Let me guess—she fell asleep."

I laughed. "You know her too well."

"She never could stay awake on a long car trip. Spent half our holidays away sleeping."

He opened the door, poking her arm. "Hey, princess. Wakey, wakey."

Rowan mumbled something, and he did it again.

She looked up, pulling off her glasses as she did so, her eyes wide as she took in her surroundings. Her face lit up with a smile as she realised who was there. "Daddy," she squealed.

Unbuckling her seatbelt, she got out the car, and jumped straight into his arms. It was pretty awesome watching them. They clearly adored one another.

It was almost as if I didn't exist as I walked behind Rowan and her father. I wandered towards the house behind them, looking around as I went. She was right about how beautiful the orchard was. From what she'd told me, it was even more beautiful in the spring, covered in blossom. I could only imagine that amazing that looked.

"Kyle," she exclaimed, letting go of her father, and grabbing my hand to pull me inside.

Her father smirked and shook his head as he stopped to take off his boots, and I just managed to kick off my shoes before heading inside this gorgeous house.

The entranceway was just as lovely as the outside, with beautiful polished wooden floors through into the living room to the side and into the kitchen at the back. As I almost slid when my socks made contact with the floor, I pictured Rowan running around this place as a kid. She must have had a ball.

Her mother stood at the kitchen bench, preparing what I assumed was going to be dinner. The house smelled as if she had been cooking for some time, the delicious aroma of roast meat floating through the air. My mouth watered at the scent. I was in for a treat.

"Rowan," the woman said warmly, turning towards us.

"Hi, Mum," Rowan said, releasing my hand to hug her.

"I put a leg of lamb in to roast for dinner, just getting everything else ready to put on when the time comes. Go and take a seat, and I'll bring you all a cup of coffee and a biscuit."

She smiled at me, leaning forward to kiss my cheek.

"You must be Kyle. We've heard all about you."

I shot a glance at Rowan, who blushed and looked at the floor. "Have you now?"

"It's all good," her mother said, patting my hand.

Rowan led me back through to the living room where her father was already waiting, leaned back in his recliner chair.

"How was the drive down?" her father asked.

She shrugged. "I slept for half of it. Pretty quiet, as far as I know."

"There wasn't a lot of traffic on the road," I said, nodding.

"I'll help you unpack the car after we've had coffee and something to eat," he said, looking at me.

"That'd be great. I only have one bag. The car is full of Rowan's stuff anyway."

He roared with laughter. "You're a good man to let her have that much space in your car. Must be a keeper."

I laughed, before looking across at Rowan. She was gaping at her father, and I wondered more than ever what she'd told them about me.

"Seriously, I know you've been a good friend to her, and after that Andrew and Charlie debacle, it's been good to hear that she's happy," he said.

"Dad," she muttered through gritted teeth.

"Sorry, pumpkin. You know me; never could keep my mouth shut." He winked, and that sealed the deal for me. He and I were going to get along famously. In fact, I could already tell this was the right place for me to be. I belonged.

FIFTEEN

ROWAN

MORTIFIED AT DAD, I wanted to crawl into a hole and hide. All my feelings for Kyle had pushed me to confiding in him and Mum about how I felt, and Dad kept hinting at it while we were talking.

After coffee, he disappeared outside with Kyle, and I watched from the window as they went to the car and began to unpack everything. My stomach churned at what he could be saying, but in no position to stop the conversation, all I could do was wait for them to come back in.

"Are you okay, Rowan?" Mum asked, as she began clearing away the coffee cups.

"I'm fine," I murmured, trying to get a better look as the two of them started laughing, my father patting Kyle on the back.

"He seems nice," she said, moving behind me.

I sighed. "He is, but you guys don't need to be so vocal about us."

She hugged me from behind. "Your father just wants to make sure he is all you say he is. He loves you, sweetheart."

"I know. Some things are just better left quiet, you know?"

"Don't tell your father next time." She laughed, going back to take the dishes to the kitchen.

I rolled my eyes, following her through to the kitchen. I opened the oven door to look at the roast lamb, breathing in its amazing smell. It wasn't worth doing something like this just for me at home, but maybe for myself and Kyle ...

"Close that door before you let all the heat out," Mum said.

"Sorry. It just smells so good." I turned and hugged her. "I'm glad to be here."

"What about tomorrow?"

I smiled. "What's done is done. They're together and happy. I've been spending time with Charlie, working through her wedding preparation. It's been nice to be with her again."

Mum nodded. "It was always a shame she couldn't spend more time here with you and Andrew. She's such a nice girl. I'm looking forward to seeing her tomorrow."

"She'll be beautiful, Mum."

She cupped my face, pressing her nose to mine. "*You* are beautiful, Rowan. Maybe that man of yours will make you finally see that."

Falling footsteps told us Dad and Kyle were back. Dad was telling Kyle just to leave my things in the hallway so I could sort them.

"They're getting on well," Mum said, "I know your father was worried you were setting yourself up for another fall. I don't think so, though."

I shrugged. "Kyle's a great friend, Mum. I don't know what I'd do without him now."

Going out to the hallway, I started sorting through my things, carrying my bag up to my room and unpacking. I went back down to find my Dad deep in conversation with Kyle in the living room. Dad was in his element, telling stories of the orchard, and I watched as they went off again on a tour round the orchard, leaving me behind.

It didn't matter, though. I smiled as I watched my two favourite men becoming friends.

AFTER DINNER, we all sat around and watched a movie. Dad and Kyle acted like old friends, and I realised Andrew had never been as comfortable as Kyle was in our house. He'd been stiff and awkward around my father, where Kyle was at ease. If our friendship ever died, I think my father would end up as devastated as I would.

I didn't realise I was staring at Kyle until he waved his hand in front of my face, waking me out of the dream I'd fallen into. The one where he loved me back; the one that I hadn't dared dream before.

"Earth to Rowan. You okay?" he asked.

"I'm fine. Probably just time for me to get some sleep. Tomorrow is a really big day."

He reached for my hand, squeezing it and smiling. "Good thinking."

I stood, moving to Dad to give him a kiss goodnight. Mum was already in bed, asleep, and I smiled at Kyle as I went to leave.

"You're all good in the spare room? Know where everything is?" I asked.

"Don't worry about me. I'll be fine. Have a good sleep, and I'll see you in the morning."

I nodded. "Goodnight."

Climbing the stairs, I paused halfway up to look at a photo on the wall. *Charlie, Andrew and I had been in our first year of high school, children verging on the edge of being adults, but we looked so carefree and happy. We'd been at Andrew's parents' beach house, and I remembered the holiday well, as Charlie had left early after becoming ill. Andrew and I spent half the summer together, left to our own devices for the most part, and that was the summer I was more sure than ever he would be mine.*

It might have been the kiss we shared while sitting under a tree, just far away enough from the house that no one would see. I shook as his hand slid down from my shoulder and touched my breast. As I gasped, he pulled his hand away, grinning at me. "Sorry, Row."

I hit his arm. "You're not sorry."

He laughed, hugging me. My stomach was awhirl with nerves, but he pulled away, grabbing at my hand to pull me towards the house. "Let's go get a drink."

All the teasing, all the flirting, none of it meant anything in the end. It didn't really matter anymore.

I kept going on to my room. Nothing had changed; all my childhood things were around the room. The narrow single bed in the corner made me ache for my queen-sized bed in my apartment. The bookcase was full of books that were tattered and falling apart, a result of rereading all my favourites over and over again.

Changing into my nightgown, I climbed into bed, and turned off the light. Tomorrow was going to be interesting.

––––––

THE SMELL of pancakes wafted through the house as I went down the stairs towards the kitchen. Mum's Saturday speciality. Kyle sat at the table, stuffing himself with food as Mum made another batch.

"Your mother's a really good cook. We can't stay here; I'll get fat," he mumbled through his mouthful.

I laughed. "Why do you think I left home?" I kissed Mum good morning, and sat at the table.

The rest of the morning was pretty uneventful as we sat around and waited. No point in getting ready too early, with the wedding being mid-afternoon. Dad was out on the orchard as usual, and Mum fretted that he'd never be ready in time, but I knew he'd be in and dressed before the rest of us. He always was.

After lunch, I went upstairs. Kyle had disappeared, and I assumed he was with Dad. I took my dress out of the wardrobe where it hung. Charlie had helped me choose it, from all those damn wedding magazines. We'd grown so close again poring over them, finding the perfect bridesmaids' dresses. They were beautiful, and I'd pictured myself wearing one. I couldn't help it.

"My sisters will look great in these, don't you think?" she'd said.

"I guess." Despite not anticipating anything, I felt a twinge of disappointment. She didn't want me.

"Now we get to find a dress that you'll look good in. Are you coming with your parents?"

That was it. And I was almost ashamed that I'd gone to bed and cried when she'd gone. She hadn't even thought of me in that way.

It was finally time to get ready. I stripped off to get changed. As I pulled off my T-shirt, it stuck on one of my earrings and I sighed as I fiddled with the fitting rather than having it rip my ear apart.

There was a tap on the door, and before I could react, I heard his voice.

"Rowan, I just wanted to see if you needed anything before we …" He stopped as he saw me, standing topless beside the bed.

I pulled my earring free, covering myself up with the T-shirt. Kyle turned his back.

"I am so, so sorry. I never would have come in if I thought you were changing."

"What did you think I was doing? Stay there while I get my dress on." I turned my back to him, letting go of the shirt to pick up the dress.

The blue chiffon floated down me as I pulled it on over my head. The fabric was soft and sensual against my skin and I revelled in the feeling before remembering Kyle was still in the room.

"You can turn around now."

He turned, and looked at me with the most intense look I'd ever seen from him. His eyes were bewildered, his breathing heavy. Maybe it was because he'd just seen me half naked; I don't know.

"Kyle? Are you okay?"

"You … you look beautiful, Rowan."

I blushed. "Thank you."

He grinned, shaking his head as if he'd just woken up. "You'll be the most beautiful bridesmaid there. I think you'll outshine the bride."

I could feel the colour draining from my face. "I'm not a bridesmaid. Where did you get that idea? I wouldn't be here if that was the case."

"Oh. I'm sorry, I just didn't think that out." Now he looked as though he'd been slapped. "I just assumed because you'd been spending all that time planning things with Charlie ... She's your friend, isn't she?"

"She has sisters." I choked back the tears as I said the words, not wanting to tell him I'd cried buckets of tears at the feeling of rejection.

A flash of anger crossed his face. "Her loss. I still get to escort the prettiest girl at the wedding."

"Charlie's gorgeous. No one is going to outshine her."

He crossed the room to take my hands in his. "I wouldn't be so sure of that."

My heart was beating fast as he looked into my eyes. He was such a good friend to me, and here I was getting tangled in the Charlie Andrew mess again. This was who I could trust now, and I felt it more than ever.

"Rowan," Mum called out from the hallway. "Do you need anything in there?"

"I'm fine, Mum," I called back.

Kyle squeezed my hands. "I have to go and get ready. See you soon, gorgeous girl."

My heart pounded at about a million beats per minute. He winked at me as he went through the door. I sat on the bed, staring at the door.

Whether he realised it or not, I was his.

SIXTEEN

KYLE

THE CAR RIDE to the wedding was silent, and I just knew Rowan was thinking about the afternoon to come. It hurt that this was breaking her heart, and I couldn't do anything about it.

What I'd seen in her room kept coming back to me. She was so beautiful, and I'd caught a glimpse of her as she'd stripped off. Seeing her made me ache to hold her in my arms and tell her how I really felt. But we had this day to get through first.

She had to see this wedding, had to see Charlie and Andrew exchange vows. Maybe then she would let go of that dream she'd had of him. All I could do was hope that happened. Until she let go, I had no hope of her seeing me as anything other than a friend.

I wanted to drive in the opposite direction, take her away from all of this, but I couldn't. I had to let this play out, no matter how much it hurt, but after this day I would not let them hurt her anymore. As far I was concerned, those two were done, and I would move heaven and earth to keep them away from her. Once today was over, that was it.

I glanced at her. She looked straight ahead, and I knew she was only just holding it together. I'd put my foot in it, assuming that Charlie had had the decency to include her best friend in the wedding party. Instead, Rowan had been left out. At least she had me.

We pulled up into the church car park, and I held her hand as we approached the building. She shook as we grew closer, holding tight as we sat in the church well behind the rows of family. There were curious looks—everyone must have known how close the three of them had been over the years—but she ignored them, staring straight ahead.

Andrew smiled and waved at her, and I wanted to get up and punch him in the face. He must have known what this was doing to her; he and Charlie supposedly knew her better than anyone. I hurt for Rowan.

I slid my arm around Rowan's shoulders, leaning over to kiss the side of her head. "You okay?"

She nodded, turning to face me. There was the tiniest of smiles on her face. Screw the people around us, I was there for her, not them.

I grinned, kissing her on the nose and squeezing her arm to show my support. When I looked up, Andrew was staring daggers at me. I just shook my head, kissing the top of Rowan's head again. If he wanted the best of both worlds, marrying Charlie and keeping Rowan dangling, I would stand in his way. No one would ever use her again.

Charlie arrived to great fanfare, and I watched as Andrew smiled at his bride.

I gripped Rowan's arm tight, and she stayed calm through the whole ceremony. While everyone threw rice, and cheered outside, we slipped back to my car.

"Are you okay, sweetheart?"

She nodded. "I can't not be okay, if that makes sense. What's done is done."

How on earth could I tell her I wanted to skip the reception? I wanted to take her home to her bed and find every freckle, explore every last inch of her body, make her scream my name. She only thought of me as a friend who was helping her through this tough situation, and all I could think about was how it would feel sinking into her, making her mine.

Instead, I drove her where she needed to be and sat with her, back from the head table. The whole situation pissed me off more and more by the minute. I got that the day wasn't about her, but I thought they could have done more for the woman they had both been best friends with since childhood.

She just looked straight ahead again, through the speeches and ate her meal without a word.

When the music started, she watched Andrew and Charlie dance, with a wistful look on her face. Her dream was over, but I wasn't finished trying to make something of the evening.

"Hey, beautiful. Want to take the next dance?" I said, leaning over to whisper in her ear.

She leaned towards me, nodding slightly.

As other couples took to the dance floor, I took her hand, pulling her to her feet. She looked so flat. "How about I show you what an amazing dancer I am?"

"Amazing, huh?" Finally a real smile broke through and she laughed, shaking her head.

"Only the best."

Her eyes lit up as I pulled her to the dance floor and into my arms, and we laughed together as we began to move. "Thank you for putting up with me today."

"That's what I'm here for Rowan. I'm certainly not here for them."

She sighed. "I know. You've been so good to me, and I must drive you nuts with the way I've been going on."

I shook my head. "This is a big deal for you. As long as you know that I'm here for you no matter what."

Rowan pulled me closer. I could smell her perfume, delicate, as she was. I didn't know if she could feel how hard I was getting, but I no longer cared. I loved this girl so freaking much, and soon I'd tell the world about it.

The hairs on my neck were standing on end, and I looked up to see Andrew staring at us. Well, looking at *me* with that pissed off look he'd had on his face before. What his problem was, I didn't know. It wasn't like he had feelings for Rowan, right?

After a couple of dances, I excused myself to go to the bathroom. If I didn't get rid of this hard-on, it could prove to be embarrassing. I closed my eyes in the bathroom cubicle, trying to get it over with as quickly as I could, the memory of seeing Rowan half naked spurring me on. What I wouldn't give to have her with me, her mouth on me.

Relieved of my burden, I left the bathroom, ready for round two. I had no idea how I would cope with the rest of the night.

Andrew was waiting for me outside.

"What the hell are you doing?" he asked.

I raised an eyebrow. Surely he didn't know what I'd just been up to. "What are you talking about?"

"Rowan is off limits. She doesn't need anyone like you around to use her and make her feel like crap."

I laughed. "Oh, really? I guess you considered her feelings when you were sneaking around with Charlie, and all but ignoring her when it came to your wedding."

"I cared about how she would feel, yes. I'm sorry she found out the way she did, but I knew she had feelings for me. She still does."

"I would say that a lot of that is gone after today. Especially tucked halfway down the church, out of the way. Would it have been too much for you and your new wife to include her? You two are supposed to be her best friends."

"We are her best friends. Which is why I'm telling you to stay away from her. I know what guys like you do to girls like Rowan."

I took a deep breath. That urge to punch him in the face? Well, it was stronger than ever right now.

"Guys like what? Guys that actually care about her? Guys that aren't you? You have no idea how much I care about Rowan. Maybe you would, if you weren't such a shitty friend to her. So you're allowed to do whatever you like with whoever you like and she gets what? Neglected? Left alone until you feel like dangling a carrot? At least she doesn't have to worry about me sneaking around behind her back, telling her lies."

He rubbed his jaw, and I wondered if I could press him enough to punch me.

"Rowan and I have been best friends since we were born. You don't get to come between us." He poked me with his index finger as if to drive the point home. I was so close to losing it with him.

"I don't need to come between you. You've driven her away. Just keep on doing what you're doing, and I can guarantee she'll want nothing more to do with you. She's not stupid, Andrew."

I turned and walked away from him. What a load of crap. On the day he dedicated his life to Charlie, here he was trying to keep Rowan tied to him too. I'd show him; I would take her away and treat her like the amazing woman she was. No lies, no holding anything back. One day we would have our own wedding, and I had no intention of inviting him or Charlie. Screw them.

Rowan stood with Charlie when I returned to the room, and I could see Charlie talking while Rowan just stood there. The light that had shone in her eyes as we danced was gone, but I saw a small smile when she spotted me heading towards them.

I grabbed hold of her, pulling her to me as I looked into those beautiful eyes. They widened in surprise and I kissed her, feeling her soft lips against mine, ignoring Charlie staring at us as I probed Rowan's mouth with my tongue.

She stiffened before relaxing in my arms, and I was sure she was kissing me in return. I ran my hand down her back until it rested just above her butt.

"Hey," I said softly, breaking away from the kiss. Her eyes were closed and when she opened them, I saw something different, new emotions. Maybe I'd broken through. I kissed her nose, grinning at the thought of more kisses like that.

"Kyle," she whispered, reaching up to touch my cheek with the palm of her hand.

I looked up at Charlie. She was gaping at what had just happened. "Congratulations, Charlie. I hope today was everything you wanted it to be."

"I ... I ... it was perfect," she stammered.

I looked back at Rowan. She had this dazed look on her face. "How about we go and get a drink."

She nodded. There was a gleam in her eye that I hadn't seen before. I hoped it was me who had put it there.

"I'm so glad you had a wonderful day, Charlie. I am so happy for you and Andrew." Rowan sounded so enthused, I could almost believe the words.

I led her away, Charlie still watching us. Her mouth hung open at what she'd witnessed, and I caught a glimpse of Andrew approaching her out of the corner of my eye, too. I couldn't wait for her to tell him what she'd seen.

We sat for a while, just drinking wine, and I was sure Rowan was acting flirty around me now. It was so hard to tell with her; she was looking at me under her eyelashes, the little smiles, and her cheeks pinking as we spoke. She looked up when the DJ announced a special song from the groom to the bride. As they started playing some old Kiss song, she looked back at the table, suddenly not so happy.

"Are you okay?" I asked.

"I'm fine."

"Want to dance again?"

She looked up, and her eyes were sad, as if she were mourning the loss of something. Chewing on her bottom lip, she looked at me for a moment before smiling. "You know, I think I might like that."

I grabbed hold of her hand, pulling her to her feet and onto the dance floor. The bride and groom both stared at us, but I ignored them, twirling Rowan around as she laughed. I pulled her closer, moving us around the room to the sound of the music. It didn't matter that anyone else was there—all I saw was her. She was happy and smiling, and so very beautiful.

When the music stopped, she closed her eyes for just a moment before breaking out into a huge smile. Opening them, she looked at me. "Thank you."

"You're welcome. Any time you want to dance, you know where to find me."

She was so close I could hear her breathing accelerate as we stood looking at each other, and I slid my hand down her back. "Kyle," she whispered.

I couldn't help it. On the dance floor I kissed her again. Her lips were warm and welcoming, and I felt her tongue press against mine in gentle, tentative moves. She had kissed me back before, and she was doing it again. Now to persuade her that I wanted to take the next step.

"That was Charlie and my favourite song when we were kids," she whispered when we broke apart, and suddenly it all made sense. The sad look when it played. It wasn't their song; it was never their song. Andrew had taken something that meant a lot to Rowan and Charlie, and taken it for them. Without realising, I had made it ours.

As we turned to step off the dance floor, Andrew and Charlie stood watching. He had that angry look on his face again, and I made sure to give him a friendly smile.

I win.

SEVENTEEN

ROWAN

THE EVENING HAD BEEN EVEN MORE amazing than I'd thought it would. When that song had started up, I couldn't believe that Andrew could do that to me. He didn't even like it, yet here he was, playing it as something special for him and Charlie. Kyle had turned the room upside down as we danced, and as he spun me around the dance floor, I laughed at the thought that we had claimed it from them.

And then he'd kissed me. Twice. In front of anyone who might be looking, and especially Andrew and Charlie. His kiss had set my body ablaze, my cheeks burning at the spectacle we must have been, my heart racing at the touch of his lips on mine.

Afterwards, he led me to the car, laughing all the way.

"Did you have a good night?" he asked.

"Better than I'd expected."

"Why was that?" We'd got to the car and we stood in the moonlight just looking at each other. Around us people were leaving, and I laughed.

"Thank you for the dancing," I said.

"Is that all?"

I rolled my eyes as he opened the car door. "I had a very pleasant evening. Thank you, Kyle."

He closed the door behind me, and walked around to the driver's side.

"You're very welcome," he said.

I didn't know what to say all the way home. I took a peek at Kyle as we drove onwards. He was whistling along with the radio and smiling at me.

Mum and Dad's car sat outside the house when we got there. They had left the wedding reception earlier, and I was keen to see what my mum thought of the whole thing.

I'd been seated well back for the wedding and reception, nowhere near the bride and groom. After all the wedding books Charlie and I had poured over, I had thought she would have included me just a little. I was so glad that Kyle had been with me. Going alone would have been the pits.

Now I wondered if the kisses had meant anything, or if he'd just done it because we had an audience. Maybe he was showing Andrew and Charlie that I didn't need them. It was all so confusing.

Mum was waiting by the door.

"I heard the car. Did you have a good night?"

I smiled. "I did, thanks, Mum."

"Goodnight, then," Kyle said, kissing me on the cheek before turning towards the stairs.

I watched him until he disappeared from sight. Today had been a good day, despite feeling as though my heart was breaking. Kyle had taken care of me like a true friend would. The kisses he'd given me had been amazing.

"So, are you going to keep that poor boy dangling?" I turned to see my mother with a big smile on her face.

"What are you talking about?"

"Anyone can see he's smitten with you, Rowan. He was attentive, and never looked at any of the other girls all night. And don't think I missed the way he kissed you."

I shrugged. "He's a good friend, Mum. He knew how hard this weekend was going to be for me."

She walked towards me. "Rowan Jean Taylor. That boy is in love with you. It's written all over his face. Honey, I know you loved Andrew, and I know you're hurt that he chose Charlie, but you have to move on. You said yourself you have feelings for Kyle. Think about what I've said. Please?"

I nodded. "Okay, Mum. I promise."

I could feel the tears welling. She was right. But Kyle? We were friends, and that was all we could ever be. He was this gorgeous, unattainable man, as far as romance goes. There was no way he felt that way about me. Maybe we were such good friends because he wasn't attracted to me. He couldn't be. Could he?

All those feelings that I held down came rising to the surface in that moment. I was the plain Jane in our group. Who would want me, with my freckles and boy body? Kyle was beautiful; there was no other way to describe him. There was no way we were compatible in that way.

"I know you want me to be happy, Mum. Kyle and I are just friends. I'm sure that's all we'll ever be. I don't think he's interested in me in that way."

How could I tell her no one like him would ever be interested in me in that way?

"I think you're crazy. You'll lose him if you're not careful, and I know you, Rowan, I know your heart. You wouldn't let him get so close if you didn't feel so much for him, and from what I can see the feeling's mutual. He worships the ground you walk on, love. See what's right in front of you before it slips away."

I stared at her for a moment, her eyes pleading with me to do what she asked. She really believed what she was saying, but she didn't know Kyle the way I did.

Turning on my heel, I ran up the stairs, away from that look. The tears flowed as I ran past the spare room door. Kyle was peeking out the doorway, and he watched as I ran past him to my room.

The calm I had felt leading up to this day ruined, I sobbed, sinking onto the floor behind my door. My dress was a mess as the tears dropped onto the fragile fabric, staining it with big, dark drops. I didn't even care if I wrecked it; the pain from the loss I'd suffered was so acute, it wiped all other concerns from my mind. Andrew and Charlie were married. I would always be on the outer with them. Even though I'd known for some time now that there was no chance for Andrew and I, the finality of this day hit hard.

I ignored the gentle tap on the door.

"Rowan, open up." Kyle's voice came from the other side. My stomach turned at the thought of what he had seen when he had walked in without knocking before.

"Rowan, let me in before your parents see me out here."

I pulled myself up on the door handle, opening the door to let him in. He stared at me as I turned my face away from him.

"What's going on? Why are you upset?"

I shook my head. "It doesn't matter anymore."

"Oh hell, Rowan. Is this about Andrew?"

I closed my eyes and shrugged. This was about Andrew, about Charlie, about me. Even about Kyle. My head was swimming with emotions and what my mother had just thrown at me.

Kyle gripped my arms, shaking me gently until I looked at him. His eyes were full of emotion, and I knew he wanted to protect me. That's what friends do for each other.

"Rowan, if this is about today and Andrew marrying Charlie, that part of your life is over. They don't deserve to have you as a friend. You are so much better than that, sweetheart. So much better than them. You would never have treated them the way they've treated you."

All I could do was to stand and look at him, trying not to sob. I couldn't find the words even to thank him for what he'd said.

"Baby, you are a beautiful woman. So smart, and sweet, and gentle. Any man would be an idiot not to be crazy in love with you. Charlie is a crap friend for not asking you to be her bridesmaid, and

Andrew is just as bad for not doing anything about it. They're not your friends, Rowan. Please tell me you see that."

I let go of the sob, collapsing into his chest as I felt his strong arms around me. I breathed in the smell of the aftershave he always wore. Safe and reassuring. At that moment, I didn't want to be anywhere else but in his embrace.

He picked me up, placing me gently on the bed and lying down beside me. There wasn't much room but I lay on my side, just looking at him while he made himself comfortable. Face to face, he stroked my cheek as the tears rolled down. His eyes seemed to search my face, looking for something. I hated him looking at me with so much pity, but I couldn't turn away.

"Don't cry. It's not worth it," he finally said.

"It just hurts so much," I whispered.

"I know it does. But, I'm here to tell you that you don't need them. Not the way you used to. You're all grown up, and need to get on with your life. Don't live in the past, Rowan."

I couldn't say anything more.

"What they did was hurtful and rude. You should have been right up the front with your friends. If not in the bridal party, then as family."

"Charlie wouldn't have wanted me in her photos," I sobbed, "I would have just ruined them."

He sighed. "Sweetheart. What makes you say that?"

"I don't fit in with them, Kyle. I never did. I was always the odd one out; it just took me a long time to see it. Andrew and Charlie are such beautiful people, and I just tagged along the whole time."

"Rowan, you are beautiful. Do you really think that little of yourself?"

I couldn't answer. If I did, the tears would start again, and I didn't know if I could stop them.

"You really have no idea just how spectacular you are. Charlie has such a generic look. You have so much more character. For what it's worth, I am crazy about your freckles."

My heart pounded as we continued to just look at each other. Could my mother be right?

"There are a lot of men out there who love the way you look. Me included. Rowan. You do these things to me I can't even begin to describe."

All the right words were coming out of his mouth, and I ached for him to kiss me, touch me. Give me what I needed. Because he needed it too.

"I don't know about that," I whispered.

"You are amazing. Andrew is an idiot for choosing Charlie. I would never make that mistake."

He rolled me onto my back, and I looked up at him. His eyes were searching my face, studying it closely, as if he were looking for something.

"I'm in love with you, Rowan. I'm so crazy about you that it drives me insane to see you so upset about someone else. I think you feel the same way, only you don't know how to tell me, or how to feel what I do. You've been so hurt and encased your heart in this cocoon that's so hard to break through. I want it; I want it all to myself. I'm no good at sharing, and Andrew made his choice."

He leaned over and kissed me, his lips pressing against mine as his tongue pushed between my teeth. I let go, closing my eyes, tentatively touching his tongue with my own.

I pushed him away, panting at the excitement of what had just happened. The kisses at the wedding were exciting, but I'd got it into my head that they were for show. This was real.

"Rowan? If you don't want me to kiss you, I'll stop. I don't want to upset you, I just want to show you how I feel."

"I do want you to kiss me. I feel like such an idiot that I didn't know how you felt. Even my mother knew."

He shook his head. "You're just you, Rowan. I wouldn't want you any other way."

That just made it even more confusing.

"What do you mean?"

"You're shy and unsure of people. It does mean that you are even more beautiful when you blush, but when you're confident you shine so bright it's blinding. I want to make you shine, Rowan. Shine for me."

The tears were building as I looked into his eyes. No one had ever said anything like this to me before, let alone meant it. Despite my instinct being to disbelieve him, and think the worst of myself, deep down I knew he meant every word.

He kissed me again, grazing my lips with his before kissing each eyelid. Kissing away my tears. Stroking my face with his palm, he grinned. "I could do this all night. There's a lot more that I want to do, too, but I don't want to fall out with your parents."

I laughed, pulling him down for another kiss. His eyes were happy, and now I knew he loved me, I saw that look too. All these years I'd never known how to read people, to know when they were being genuine. Now I could read Kyle's face, and he was all mine. Now was the time for me to be open and honest with him.

"I have to tell you something," I whispered. He frowned, his brows furrowing in concern.

"What's wrong?"

"Nothing. It's just that I haven't been with anyone before."

He cocked an eyebrow at that. "I thought you'd had other relationships."

"I did. Kind of. I just never got as far as sleeping with someone." He stroked my forehead with his palm, and it gave me comfort after telling him the biggest secret I had. Who on earth confesses to being a virgin at twenty-two?

His kisses were gentle, his lips soft as he began to kiss my face again, my lips, my nose, and my cheeks. As he trailed kisses down my neck, I felt his hand stroke my shoulder, moving down to cup my breast.

Without thinking about it, I froze, and he withdrew his hand.

"Sorry, baby. I should slow down, I'm just excited about being with you."

"I just feel really self-conscious."

"I love you, Rowan. Your body has been driving me crazy all these weeks."

I laughed, and he nuzzled my nose. "We'll go at what pace you want. As long as I know you love me too."

"I do," I whispered. And it was true. I'd been attracted to him from the start, but the past few weeks I was sure I'd ended up with another case of unrequited love.

"Good. I want so much to touch you, make up for the weeks we could have been in your bed instead of on your couch."

All that did was make me laugh again, and he raised his finger to his lips to shush me. "Your dad will throw me out if he finds out I'm in here."

"I am a grown-up." I grinned at him.

"I know, but if I ever have to come back here to visit or for any other reason, I'd really rather he didn't greet me with a shotgun."

I stifled a giggle. He ran his hand down from my shoulder again, and I gasped as his thumb grazed my nipple before he reached for my hand.

"You okay?" he asked, clearly oblivious to what he'd done.

"I'm fine. Just self-conscious about parts of my body."

"What parts? They all look good to me."

"I've never had any boobs. You've seen Charlie. Compared to her I'm like a surfboard."

He rolled his eyes. "After what I saw today, I'd beg to differ. In fact, I would probably freak you out if I told you how much I'd been thinking about your boobs earlier."

I stared at him, slapping him on the arm and laughing. The blush burned on my cheeks. "You did not."

"Dancing so close to you dressed like this had some side effects. I had to go and relieve myself."

My mouth had fallen open at what he was saying, and he laughed as he kissed my nose.

"You are adorable," he said.

He looked so sweet and sincere. My body had just reacted to him in a most unexpected way. I'd always dreamed that Andrew would be my first, my last, my everything. Now, this gorgeous man wanted to be with me. I'd been surprised enough that he'd wanted to be friends. Now he wanted more.

"One step at a time. This weekend has just been just a mind-fuck."

He grinned. "Anything you want. Now, are you going to let me kiss you some more?"

My heart felt as if it would explode as I nodded. Somehow his tongue found its way into my mouth again, though this time I was prepared and kissed him back.

He groaned, pressing his body to mine, and I felt him harden against me. No one had ever made me feel this way. I wanted him between my legs so badly, but I'd just told him I wanted to take it slow.

"Rowan," he whispered, kissing me again. "I could kiss you all night."

"I could let you kiss me all night," I whispered back, grinning.

"You know I have this fantasy of finding every damn freckle on your body."

I giggled as he kissed my neck. This felt amazing. I'd wanted Andrew to pay attention to me for so long, always putting him first, completely neglecting my own needs. Now Kyle wanted to take care of those needs, the same ones it appeared he'd just woken up.

"You know, we could have sex if you wanted to," I said.

He froze, pushing himself up to look at me.

"Is that what you really want? Or what you think I want?"

I shrugged. "I don't know. Both?"

"Apart from the fact that this bed is so narrow, and I want to do things to you that might need more space, if it's going to be your first time it needs to be special."

I stroked his cheek, his words speaking volumes for the esteem he held me in. He didn't just want sex, he wanted more. Why hadn't I seen this before? I'd wasted so much time just being friends when I could have given him my heart.

"Okay," I whispered, "I have no idea what I'm doing, but I'm sure you've worked that out."

He laughed, kissing me tenderly. "I should go back to my room and let you get some sleep. Before you tempt me into anything more."

I nodded.

"We can just do what feels right. As much as I would love for us to rut like rabbits right now, we need to be somewhere not under your parents' roof."

I sighed. "You're right. I did say that myself."

"So, I am going to leave you here with that thought, and go and take care of myself before going to sleep."

He kissed me on the nose, standing up beside the bed and looking down at me. "I don't think I've jacked off twice in one day since I was a teenager. In fact, I don't think I've done it so much than since I met you. How's that for a final thought before bed?"

I laughed as he left the room, throwing a pillow a the door. I closed my eyes, unable to believe what had just happened. For the first time in so long, I had stopped thinking of Andrew and Charlie and the miserable time that I'd had. Now I had something to look forward to. Something real.

EIGHTEEN

KYLE

I LEFT Rowan's room and climbed into my own bed, still thinking of how things had gone. Now she knew how I felt and best of all, wanted to take things further.

She was so fragile, especially after the day's events. While I wanted to strip that gorgeous dress off her, I had to take baby steps. She had been put through enough by those selfish 'friends' of hers, so if it meant taking our time, I would do whatever it took to make her happy.

Normally, I would jump in feet first, but that might be too much for her. Especially with her so recently broken-hearted over this marriage. At least now she could move on.

In the morning, she was at the kitchen table when I made my way down for breakfast. She lit up when I approached, and I leaned over to kiss her softly before sitting down. Her mother had a look on her face that I could only describe as an 'I told you so' look.

Rowan rolled her eyes before pouring me a coffee.

"You don't have to do that, Rowan."

"I know. I want to." She smiled at me, and I couldn't help but grin at the twinkle in her eye. I'd seen her happy, but now she was alive, and I loved that I was responsible for that look. She was finally freed from the crap of her past, and ready to love me.

"Are you two going back today?" Rowan's father asked.

"Yeah," she said, "I've got work tomorrow, and I didn't want to take time off in the middle of the project I'm working on."

"It's been good to see you, Rowan. You should come home more often."

"Yes, Dad," she said, squeezing my thigh under the table.

I fought back the laugh at her bold behaviour. Yesterday, she would never have been so forward. Maybe we wouldn't take things as slowly as I thought.

"I was surprised you drove down. Would have been faster to fly."

"Kyle hadn't been down this way before. We thought we'd take the scenic route." She reached for another piece of toast, and buttered it before placing it on my plate. Out of the corner of my eye, I saw her father raise an eyebrow. Something had changed between us since yesterday, and he knew it.

"We had a good drive down," I said. "We're going back a different way. Along the coast."

He nodded. "I know the road. Perfect day for a drive, too. Travel safely, you two."

I just smiled at him, not quite prepared to sit down with her father to talk about her future with me. We had to work that out between us first. "I'll take care of her," I said, and he nodded, holding eye contact as he did. It was as good as a promise.

———

WE LEFT JUST AFTER LUNCH, giving Rowan as much time with her parents as we could before the six-hour drive home. Her parents kissed her goodbye as we left, and her father came around my side of the car to shake my hand.

"She likes you. Just be good to her."

"I promise," I said. He shook my hand and took a deep breath, glancing over at Rowan who was talking to her mother. "Kyle, she feels everything, and hides nothing once you know what to look for. You're the first man outside of Andrew who seems to genuinely care for her, and that means a lot, but she's precious and more fragile than she seems at times."

I nodded, not wanting to get into an argument and point out that if anything, I think I cared more for Rowan than Andrew did. Especially after the way she'd been sidelined at the wedding.

"She's very special to me, Mr Taylor. We'll just see how things go."

He seemed happy with that, smiling as I sat in the car. He bent at the open window. "She's a smart one, just naive at times. All she's ever really wanted was to be loved."

"That's the easy part," I said before realising what I'd admitted to.

He stood, clearly happy with my response, and I watched as Rowan ran around the car to him for one last hug. She really was so sweet, and the thought of taking her home and being with her made me anxious to leave.

The road was quiet, and with the weather being hot and sunny, we had the windows down to let a gentle breeze blow through the car. Rowan couldn't stop smiling, and I knew I was the reason behind it. We made small talk about the scenery, the conversation littered with laughter and those shy smiles that did so much for me. Every so often, she'd place her hand over mine on the gear stick, and look at me through those long eyelashes of hers.

"Love you," I said, and she would grin, her face lighting up at the words I'd held in for so long.

She leaned back in her seat, putting her feet on the dashboard while she played a game on her phone. I reached over, playfully slapping her ankle to tell her to put her feet down.

"Spoil sport," she said.

"I'm just looking out for your safety, like I promised your father."

She cocked an eyebrow, twisting her mouth, and I just knew she was dying to ask what else I'd said to him.

"He wanted me to look out for you, Rowan. You know, seeing as we're together now, and you didn't really hide it this morning at breakfast."

The smile crept back across her face, and she blushed. "I'm happy, and I want everyone to know it."

"We will tell the world, baby. I want everyone to know you're all mine." She placed her hand across her mouth to stifle a giggle. "You don't have to hide how you feel, Rowan. Not with me."

Rowan leaned over, planting a kiss on my cheek. "I love you too," she said, nuzzling my face.

"Stop that," I said with a laugh. "I need the blood to go to my brain in order to drive and not have an accident."

She giggled, sitting back in her seat, her eyes widening as we drew close to somewhere she clearly recognised. "We used to come here as kids. That road leads to the beach."

"Do you want to stop and take a look?"

Rowan shook her head. "We used to go there every weekend. Andrew's parents owned a house not far from the beach, but they sold it years ago. I just want to go home now and get on with my new life. Our new life." She smiled, resting her head back on the headrest. "I'll try not to fall asleep this time."

Despite her words, the gentle curves on the road soon sent her off to sleep, and when we arrived I unpacked the car, gently waking her to take her and her things up to her apartment.

Her eyes were still so heavy, and I helped her into her bedroom where she curled up on the bed, falling back asleep in an instant.

I smiled, pulling the blanket over her and kissing her on the forehead. "Sleep well, gorgeous," I whispered. "See you at work tomorrow."

She murmured something in her sleep—I think it was goodbye—and I left for home to spend another night alone. Although now, I knew those nights were numbered.

She loved me.

NINETEEN

KYLE

I'D TOLD my father about Rowan and me when I got home, and laughed when he really wasn't surprised.

"You two have been spending so much time together, it was only a matter of time," he said, not even looking up from his newspaper.

"And you're okay with that?"

He looked up at me and smiled. "I don't think I could stop either of you if I tried. If it causes any issues at work, then we'll be talking about it again, but if it makes you happy, Kyle, then I'm happy."

"She's awesome, Dad, she really is. When you get to know her better you'll see just how amazing she is."

"From what I've seen of her, I'm sure you're right. There have been a few bumps, but I'd be sorry to see her go."

I grinned. That was as close to a blessing as I was going to get from him, but it'd do. He would be concerned about any relationship I entered into after the last one, but this was different; Rowan was different.

After showering, I planted myself on the couch in front of the television. All the travel had tired me out, and I was ready to collapse into my bed, if I didn't fall asleep where I was.

My phone buzzed after a couple of hours, jolting me from dozing. I yawned, picking it up, and smiling at the text from Rowan.

> Sorry I fell asleep. See you for coffee in the morning?

I grinned. If I hadn't been dead on my feet, I would have gone back over to her place, but I wouldn't have been much use to her.

> Sure thing. Have a good sleep. I love you, pretty lady.

I stood. Dad was asleep in his recliner chair, his snoring getting louder and louder as he fell deeper into sleep. I covered him with a blanket and headed off to bed. My phone buzzed again.

> I love you too. Sleep well.

Smiling, I climbed into my cold bed. Declaring our feelings was a start; now we could build a life together.

I held her heart in the palm of my hand, knowing that the slightest discouragement could shatter it into a million tiny pieces. She was so sensitive, but I would do whatever it took not to break her, ever, not even accidentally.

My head was so full of Rowan, I thought I'd have trouble sleeping, but that turned out not to be a problem after all.

SHE WAS ALREADY at work when I got there, which wasn't unusual, but instead of greeting me bright and happy as I'd thought she would, she was looking worried and buried in her computer.

"Hey," I said.

Rowan looked up, and it took a moment for her to smile. She seemed too distracted to even realise it was me.

"What's up?" I sat on the other side of her desk and she shook her head.

"Just busy. Your father has asked me to go over all the systems and make sure they're all working as they should be. It came as a bit of a surprise after everything that's happened, but I want to do a thorough job, and show him I know what I'm doing."

I leaned forward. "Rowan, he wouldn't ask you to do it if he didn't think you were capable. Despite what's happened, he does still have faith in you."

She frowned. "It's not because we're together now, is it? I mean, he's not trying to favour me because of us?"

"That's not how my father works. If anything, us being together will probably make things more difficult. I think it means he's worried and does have doubts about what Ross told him. This is a good thing, sweetheart."

She was chewing her bottom lip, and I raised an eyebrow at what that meant. Usually there were words she didn't want to say, and I knew I wasn't going to like it.

"This is going to keep me busy for the next few days. I know we were going to spend time together, but I have to get this done."

I rolled my eyes. "I think I know you well enough to know that you are going to be focused on this until it's finished. Maybe I can come around to your place and feel you up while you work? I could even get under the desk right now."

She laughed loudly, clamping her hand across her mouth at the noise.

"Seriously. I'll go get you a coffee if you want one, and you get on with it. The sooner you finish, the sooner I get to have my wicked way with you."

Shaking her head and laughing, she went back to her work, and I left to get her a coffee. Dad was in the staff room when I went in, and he smirked at the sight of me making two cups of coffee.

"And so it begins," he said, nudging my arm.

"What?"

"Being at Rowan's beck and call."

"It's not like that, it's …" He laughed, teasing me, and I looked down, shaking my head.

"Well, given that you've thrown enough work at her to keep us apart for days, I'm just trying to do something nice for my girlfriend."

"Girlfriend, huh?" Miriam's voice came from behind and I picked up the cups to head back to Rowan's office. There were a few people milling around now, and I knew if I didn't make a stand the gossip mill would be making stuff up.

"Yes, Miriam. Rowan is my girlfriend. So you don't have to worry about me hassling her anymore. Turns out she likes it."

She laughed, and smiled as I walked away. I knew that word would spread pretty fast as I walked past a couple of the sales reps in the hallway. One of them had been very flirtatious with me since I'd been back. She would have heard my words, and maybe now she'd leave me alone.

Despite Rowan being buried in her new project, there was still a spring in my step as I made my way back to her office.

When I passed Ross in the corridor, he was muttering under his breath, scowling as he walked past. "You okay, Ross?" I asked brightly, not really caring about the answer.

He glared at me. "I hear that girl is checking up on me. I suppose you have something to do with it."

"If 'that girl' is Rowan, it has nothing to do with me. Entirely Dad. Maybe he's realised she's a lot more capable than you've allowed her to demonstrate so far."

"I didn't need help for this project, let alone from a girl," he growled. I was pretty sure the throbbing vein on his forehead was going to pop as he spewed his venom.

"Oh, is that what your problem is? A newly graduated young woman is smarter than you are?" I put on the most innocent face I could as he stormed off. I laughed as he disappeared around the corner. Dad must have really upset him for him to be so open in his disdain for Rowan.

That answered that question, though. He must have not been happy with Dad's hiring decision. She'd done the work he couldn't do, and he wanted rid of her. Dad's decision had thrown him enough to lose the plot. Good job, he deserved it.

If anything I had a bigger smile on my face when I delivered Rowan's coffee. She looked up, raising an eyebrow at me. "What's going on?"

"Why do you ask?"

"Because you look like the cat that got the cream. What are you up to?"

"Nothing, pretty lady. Just love you heaps, that's all."

She grinned, shaking her head. "I guess I can let you have that one."

SHE LEANED cross-legged against the doorframe, and I was so focused on what I was doing, I didn't notice her at first.

"Ahem." She cleared her throat, grinning as I looked up.

"Hey. What's up?"

"So I need an excuse to come and visit you now?"

I laughed. "Come here, and I'll show you how happy I am to see you.

She crossed the room, and I turned back from my desk as she straddled my legs to sit facing me.

"You are very forward today, Miss Taylor," I said, pulling her down for a kiss.

When we broke apart, her eyes were closed, her face showing the simple peace we both felt being together.

"I finished my report for your father. Just delivered it. Three days of constant work has driven me a bit crazy, but I'm free now.

I hugged her tight. "Well done."

She shrugged. "I voiced my concerns about a few things. Ross hasn't screwed up too much yet, but I do worry that he will."

"It is what it is, sweetheart. If you ask me, he's jealous of you. Young and talented. You're destined for bigger things, Rowan, and he's stuck in his ways."

She clung on round my neck, and I closed my eyes, just breathing her in. We'd not had many chances for intimate moments since we'd gotten back, and this wasn't the time or the place, but I didn't know if I cared.

"Do you want to come to my place tonight?" she said, leaning back again.

"I would love to. As long as you're not going to fall asleep on me."

Rowan shook her head. "I worked hard to get the report done so we could relax together. I'll cook dinner, and we might even open a bottle of wine. Though you'll have to sort that bit out, as I know nothing about it."

I laughed. "I think I can manage that."

She bent her head for another kiss before leaping from my lap.

"Oh, you mean I don't have to work all afternoon with you sitting there? I was kind of enjoying the view."

Rowan smiled shyly, rocking side to side. "Maybe you can have more of a view tonight."

I cocked an eyebrow at her words. "I look forward to it. Have a good afternoon."

SHE WAS A GREAT COOK, just like her mother, and I pictured her learning to cook in that big, old, kitchen. Her only frustration was using dry pasta to make her spaghetti dish. Apparently her mother made her own. That didn't lessen the taste, and the food was infused with basil and oregano, smelling great and tasting amazing.

"You can cook for me any time," I said, laughing.

"Happy to," she said proudly.

I reached across the table, grabbing her hand in mine and squeezing. "This is perfect. I love you."

"I love you too. Sorry I've been so busy."

I laughed. "I know how focused you can get, and I knew once you were finished, you'd be all mine."

She smiled. "I am."

When we'd finished eating, she cleared the plates. I could hear water running from the kitchen. I moved behind her, wrapping my arms around her waist.

"What are you doing?" I asked.

"Washing the dishes."

I kissed her neck, and she sighed, her body relaxing against mine.

"I just want the kitchen to be tidy," she grumbled.

"Plenty of time to do that. I want you on the couch with me. We can snuggle while watching TV and see where it leads us."

Her breathing grew heavier as she leaned back against me.

"Rowan," I whispered, pulling at her waist until she turned and looked at me. Eye to eye, we looked at each other for a moment, before I leaned forward, grazing her lips with mine.

She nodded, leaving the dishes in the sink and following me into the living room and sitting on the couch. I picked up the remote, flicking through the channels until I found a movie that looked good. Not that we were really going to watch it.

I leaned back, pulling her into my arms and lifting her chin with my finger to look into her eyes. What she couldn't say with words, I could see in her face. I kissed her, finding her tongue with mine, her body relaxing as our kiss grew more intense.

Laughing softly, I moved to rest my head on the arm of the couch, beckoning her to lie beside me. She pounced, grinning as she snuggled in.

Squeezed together on the couch, this was it, finally she was all mine. I would take her to bed and make her forget anyone else she'd ever looked at sideways. We would be everything to each other, and I would explore that gorgeous body of hers so slowly, she would moan at the thought of my touch.

Her eyes lit up when I stroked the hard nipple through the fabric.

"Kyle," she whispered, but didn't move my hand away.

I grinned. "It's okay, baby. We'll go as slow or as fast as you want."

"Slow," she whispered, rolling on top of me, grinding her pelvis against mine. I was so damn hard, it was a miracle my pants were still in one piece.

"Anything you want." I kissed her, tasting her tongue. Her body pressed hard against mine, I wanted to savour every inch. Her neck tasted just as good, and she moaned, running her hands down my back as I took tiny nips of her skin.

"God, I want you so bad. Always did," I murmured.

I felt her jump as the phone rang beside us. "You have got to be kidding me." I laughed, kissing her on the nose.

A moment of indecision crossed her face. "Rowan, if you need to answer it, just do it. I'm not going anywhere."

She smiled, reaching for the phone. "Sorry. No one ever calls. It might be important."

I nuzzled her neck as she rolled off me to answer, before I sat up to watch her.

"Hi, Mum." She rolled her eyes at me, waving her hand as if trying to speed up the conversation. I went back to her neck, planting kisses up toward her ear as I tried my best to distract her.

She gasped, and I sat back up again. She shook, tears welling in her eyes, and her mouth hung open as she sat in silence, listening to whatever her mother was saying.

"Rowan?"

"I can't believe it," she said into the phone. "Not Charlie."

Now I was worried. Something had happened.

"I'll be okay. Kyle's with me. Thanks, Mum." Her voice shook. She hung up and just stared at the phone.

"Rowan? What's wrong? What's happened?"

She looked up at me, her eyes filled with tears. They ran down her face, leaving a trail behind them. I just wanted to kiss them away, but first I needed to know what was causing them.

"Charlie's dead." She struggled for breath as she sobbed the words out.

"What?"

"She ... she had an asthma attack. A big one. It had been so long. Mum said they got her to the hospital, but it was too late."

I ran my fingers through my hair. This was unbelievable.

"Shit. Oh, sweetheart, come here."

She threw her arms around my neck, clinging to me as she sobbed. I held her as tight as I could, stroking her hair as she let it all out. My poor girl; she had already been through so much and now, as she had come out the other side and found happiness with me, she was back in that hole she had dug herself out of.

If I knew her at all, I knew she'd feel guilty at being envious of Charlie, at falling out with her, at feeling left out at the wedding. None of that was fair because they hadn't been fair to her. The trick was making her see that.

We sat, entangled in each other until she fell asleep in my arms. Tonight had been the night we were going to make love for the first time. Instead, I carried my devastated girlfriend to bed, where I placed her gently between the sheets before stripping down and climbing in beside her.

When I put my arm over her, she nestled into me. She snuggled up so close, and all I wanted to do was kiss her and take her pain away. I watched her sleep until I was too tired to keep my eyes open. This was going to be tough to get through, but whatever she needed from me, it was hers.

IN THE MORNING, she was still asleep when I woke, and I traced a pattern through her freckles until her eyes flickered open. She smiled at me, still half-asleep. "Good morning," she murmured.

"Good morning." I kissed her tenderly, and she wrapped her leg around mine, pulling me towards her.

I laughed, raising an eyebrow. "What are you up to?"

"You're warm."

Her face changed as the memory of the night before hit, and I could see the grief in her eyes as she lay there, just looking at me.

"It really happened, didn't it?"

I nodded. "It did, sweetheart."

"I just can't imagine a world without Charlie in it. And on their honeymoon. Andrew must be devastated."

I put my palm to her cheek. "I'm sure he is. Come here."

She moved into my arms, and I kissed her deeply, her hand stroking my hair.

"I'm glad you're here," she whispered, kissing my chest.

"I wouldn't be anywhere else right now. Rowan, whatever you need, I'm here."

She looked up at me. Her eyes were so sad and I just wanted to kiss the pain away. "I just need you."

And then she began to cry again.

TWENTY

ROWAN

I FELT EMPTY. Like there was nothing left to feel inside; I'd used up all my emotions and had nothing left to give. My life had gone from this joyous discovery that Kyle loved me, and that we were going to be happy, to the depths of depression as my heart broke with Charlie's death.

Poor Kyle. We were so close to making love for the first time, and that phone call had changed everything. But how could it not?

My Charlie was dead.

The time I'd spent with her before the wedding meant all the more to me now. We had renewed our friendship, even if I'd felt left out at the event itself. She cared enough to ask me my opinion when it mattered to her, and now she would never be able to return the favour.

I was lost in a sea of grief, and the only person who truly understood was Andrew. He was as broken-hearted as I was, and we started spending time together as we both recovered from our terrible loss.

Kyle stood by me through the funeral. He held me when I cried, and loved me, even though there was more distance between us than there was when we'd first met. This was as hard on him as it was on me, and our relationship came to a grinding halt rather than advancing as it had been.

We would get through this together. Despite everything, our love had grown all this time, and was solid enough that nothing could shake it.

Kyle was so sweet and understanding as I spent more time with Andrew, helping him adjust to a life without Charlie.

But that had to end; Andrew had to take care of himself. I had my own life to get on with.

THREE WEEKS HAD PASSED since Charlie had died, and I still couldn't reconcile my thoughts. We'd had our ups and downs, but I still loved her. In the end, I always would.

Being busy at work helped keep my mind off things, but when I got home, I'd wallow in self-pity, or go and see Andrew, who was suffering so much.

Kyle and I would catch up over coffee in the mornings, and he brought the only sunshine into my life. His frustration was obvious, and I was painfully aware there had to be an end to his patience, but I was in such a black hole, the other side was to hard to see. I had to shake it off somehow, and yet it was just so hard. Dad always said I felt everything so deeply, and this was the most difficult thing I'd ever been through.

When Kyle didn't turn up for coffee, I went looking for him. He was so punctual, so attentive, it worried me that he hadn't come.

He sat in the lunch room, laughing at something that Angela, the hot sales rep, had said. I watched as she sat across the table, flicking her hair through her hands as she flirted with my boyfriend. A searing hot pain stabbed my chest, as I watched. What if he was no better than any other man? My heart in torment, I wanted to run away, but something kept me there, mesmerised as this beautiful woman teased and joked with the man I was in love with.

Turning away, I took a deep breath. *I want to go back to my office to cry.* That's how I would have handled it before Kyle, but now? I exhaled, closing my eyes and summoning the courage to enter the room. He was worth fighting for; we were worth it.

He turned as I came in the door, and the smile in his eyes told me everything I needed to know. I was panicking over nothing.

"Hey, beautiful," he said, his entire focus on me. Angela stopped mid-sentence, staring at me with such disdain that my torment turned to satisfaction. He was mine.

"I went to make our coffee, but the machine needed to do its cleaning cycle first. It's just about finished." He reached for me, pulling me towards him and wrapping his arms around my waist. My heart pounded as I bent to kiss him.

"What have you been doing this morning?" he asked.

"Taking a look at an update for the new system. I'll be putting it in place after everyone goes home," I said.

He grinned. "We can talk tonight. I'll make dinner if you want to sample my cooking. I hear it's pretty good."

"Let's get coffee and go back to my office."

"Anything you want." His eyes were fixed on me as if I were the only person in the room. Angela sat, forgotten on the other side of the table, and just looked awkward, as if she were interrupting something.

I carried the coffee back to my office, placing it on the desk so I could hug Kyle. In his arms, I felt safe, all my earlier fears gone as his love was on display, right in front of me.

"I've missed you," he whispered. "Meeting for coffee isn't enough."

"I know. The past few weeks have been so tough, but I'm not going to make myself better by neglecting you. Not when I love you so much," I said, squeezing him tight.

"I just needed to hear those words." He smelled so good, that musky scent of his aftershave so familiar, I just wanted to lose myself in him. Now we could get back on track, and *that* would finally happen. It felt like we'd been waiting forever.

"So, dinner tonight?" he asked.

"Yes, but a bit later than normal dinnertime, if that's okay. Once I get this update out of the way."

"You could show up at midnight and I'd be ready and waiting for you," he said, laughing. "I just want us to get our shit together."

"I just want to get back to how we were. I never meant to neglect you."

Kyle lifted his hand to my face, stroking my cheek as I closed my eyes. "I love you, Rowan. More than I ever thought was possible. Through everything, I know I can depend on you, that your heart belongs to me."

I nodded.

"As mine belongs to you," he whispered, lifting my face to kiss me. I opened my eyes to his. They were smiling, and telling stories of his love for me.

No more words required.

TWENTY-ONE

ROWAN

I ENDED up working later than I'd expected, as everything went so slowly. I kept calling Kyle to update him, and he sounded more and more tired, but was so understanding.

Finally, I got out just after 10pm, and raced to his place. He wasn't answering his phone, and I assumed he'd left it somewhere random. It wouldn't have been the first time. I knocked on the door, and when there was no answer, I unlocked it with the key he'd given me.

He was fast asleep on the couch, snoring softly. I shook my head, smiling. He looked so comfortable, I couldn't bear to wake him. I shook my head, remembering how I'd fallen asleep on the way home from the wedding. He'd taken care of me then, as I would take care of him now.

I went to his bedroom, and grabbed a blanket from the bed. It smelled of him, and I held it up, inhaling his scent, and smiling as I placed it over his body.

Maybe tonight hadn't worked out how we'd planned, but there were plenty of other nights to come. Dinner was already in the refrigerator; it would keep until tomorrow when I made it up to him. I fished a pen out of my bag, found a napkin and wrote him a note to let him know I had shown up. For a moment, I tossed up whether to just hop in his bed, but I was tired and wanted to shower, not to mention that all my clean clothes were back at my apartment. At least it wasn't far to go home.

I hadn't been home long when there was a knock on the door. I grinned, thinking of Kyle waking and reading the note. Maybe he couldn't wait until the morning.

Andrew stood in the doorway, looking tired and disheveled. "Can I come in, Row?"

"I guess. Sure."

I hid my disappointment as I let him in.

He sat on the couch as I went to the kitchen to make coffee. "Want one?"

"That'd be great," he said. "Hey, can I crash here? I hate being in the apartment without Charlie, and a change of scene for the night might help."

"Um yeah, sure. You can sleep on the couch."

He smiled. "Thanks. I really appreciate it."

Following me into the kitchen, he stood behind me while I made coffee. "How are you doing?" he asked.

"I'm okay. Trying to get back to normal."

"I don't know if anything will ever be normal again," he said.

I handed him his coffee, leading him back to the living room. Sitting on the couch, I sighed as I took a sip, relieved to be finished work for the day, but missing Kyle.

"Are you still with Kyle?" he asked. These past weeks, we'd barely talked about anything other than Charlie.

I nodded. "We were meant to have this evening together, but I ended up working. I'll see him tomorrow."

"Is he good to you, Row?" He looked so sad as he asked.

"He's amazing. Loves me a lot."

We sat and sipped our coffee in silence, and when it was gone, I stood, taking his cup and placing them in the kitchen sink.

I left him with a pillow and a blanket, and climbed into bed for a good night's sleep. My mind drifted to Kyle; his hand on my breast, telling me how beautiful I was ... No one had ever done that. If only the work this evening had gone smoother, maybe I would be at his place in bed with him right now.

Reaching between my legs, I stroked my clit, rubbing it as I thought of him touching me. I stroked my breast with my free hand, feeling the nipple come to life at the thought of that man making love to me.

"Rowan?"

I froze. The blankets were over me, so he couldn't have seen what I was doing. *Shit.*

"I can't sleep. I keep thinking about Charlie. Can I get in bed with you?"

"Andrew, I don't think that's a good idea."

He climbed in beside me before I could protest. "I'll stay over this side, I promise."

I rolled over and looked at the clock. It was after midnight. I should call Kyle to let him know Andrew was here, but he would probably still be fast asleep.

"Fine, whatever. But you stay on that side of the bed."

I kept my back to him, staying as far to the edge of the bed as possible. Before long, I felt his arm over me, as he pulled me back towards him.

"Rowan."

Reluctantly, I turned onto my back to look at him. There was moonlight coming through a gap in the curtain, and I could see the tears on his cheeks.

"I miss her so much," he said.

"I know. I miss her too."

Before I could process what he was doing, he was on top of me, his tongue in my mouth, and I pushed him as hard as I could. He was heavy, and in a panic, I slid out from underneath him.

"Get off me," I screeched, breaking away and leaping out of bed.

"Your wife has only been dead a few weeks." My heart raced, and I held my hands up to show him to stay away.

"I need you, Rowan. I need you to help me feel better. I know you love me." He was on his knees, crawling towards me.

I shook my head, walking out to the living room to get on the couch myself.

"Rowan?"

"Just go the fuck to sleep, Andrew. You can leave in the morning."

I RUBBED MY EYES, trying to get rid of that first-thing-in-the-morning blurriness. I'd been woken by a knock on the door, and whoever it was knocked again before I got there.

Kyle stood in the doorway with a bag of bagels in one hand and flowers in the other.

"I thought seeing as we missed each other last night, I'd treat you to breakfast."

I laughed. "That sounds great."

And then his eyes weren't smiling anymore as the flowers and bagels dropped to the floor. He wasn't even looking at me, but over my shoulder. Confused, I stared at him. "Are you okay?"

I turned. Andrew stood in the doorway of my bedroom, clad only in boxers.

"What the hell?" Kyle said.

"It's not what it looks like," I said. But Kyle wasn't even listening to me.

"Hey, Row, are you coming back to bed?" Andrew smirked, and I shot him the filthiest look I could muster.

"You are disgusting," I said. "Kyle, please. I slept on the couch. We didn't even ..."

I turned back towards the door. He was gone.

"Shit." I ran out to the lifts, pressing the buttons wildly to follow him. Why is it that when you're in a hurry, the elevator never comes? It seemed to take forever to get to the building lobby, and I ran out to the front of the building, dressed in my nightgown and trying to find the man I loved.

"Kyle," I yelled, unable to see him anywhere. He was gone, and my whole world crumbled beneath me. I felt ill at what he'd seen, what he believed had happened. Andrew hadn't helped. As soon as I was back upstairs, he would be gone from my life. For good.

I ran back inside, ignoring Andrew and digging through my bag for my mobile. I hit redial; the only person I called these days was Kyle, but all it did was ring until it went to voicemail.

"Hey, please call me when you get this. It wasn't what it looked like. I need to talk to you and hear you're okay. Please call me, Kyle. I love you."

I felt Andrew's hand on my shoulder. "If he loved you, he would have waited for an explanation."

Never in my life had I felt so much rage. It ran over me like a hot wash and I could feel my body tensing with the anger building in me.

"Get the fuck out of my apartment; get out of my life. I don't ever want you near me again," I screamed.

He went pale, backing away from me as I spat the words.

"This isn't you, Row. Look at what's happened to you since you've been with him. You never used to act like this, talk like this. I don't think I've ever heard you say a bad word in your life."

"I was loved," I yelled. "I was loved and wanted, which is more than you ever gave me. All I got from you was teasing, and I was stupid enough to fall for it. All these years you never wanted me; you still don't want me. You're just trying to fill the gap. I am sorry that Charlie died, I loved her too. But I am not going to just run when you click your fingers. Not anymore."

I tried to breathe through the tears that were falling. He just stood there, looking at me as if he didn't know me, and I realised he never really knew me at all. All those years I had been in love with the dream of him. The real Andrew wasn't what I wanted.

All my life I wanted to be what Charlie was. Beautiful. I never felt that way when it was the three of us. Only Kyle had ever made me see a side of myself I didn't know about. Kyle made me feel as if I were the most beautiful woman in the world, and he was my future. If he didn't call me back I didn't know what I would do.

Finally, Andrew turned back towards the bedroom to get changed, leaving without a further word while I rocked on the couch. Loving Andrew had screwed up my life. Now, just when I was moving on and starting something new, he had screwed that up.

I felt nothing for him.

TWENTY-TWO

ROWAN

ALL MORNING, the world went on around me while I sat in my office, staring at nothing. I had gone looking for Kyle when I came in, but there was no sign of him, and no one knew where he was. He was out there, somewhere, thinking that I had cheated on him. My heart ached at the thought of the pain he was feeling. I felt it too.

I didn't even hear the knock on the door at first, the sound of the door opening jolting me back to reality.

"Mr Warner wants to see you." Miriam stood there, a quizzical look on her face.

"Kyle?"

"No, Warner Senior."

I had that horrible sinking feeling where you know the end is coming, but you don't know what form it will take. That was me. This was too much of a coincidence, after last night.

Slowly, I stood, making my way to the other side of the building where the executive offices were. I had already been over here once this morning, looking for Kyle. As I went past his office, I wanted to open the door and check again, but I knew he wouldn't be there.

"Rowan, take a seat." John Warner indicated the seat opposite his desk and I sat down, gripping the base of the chair to bolster my nerves.

"I'm going to get straight to the point. There are some efficiencies we will be making throughout the business. We believe that we can streamline things by restructuring. Now several big projects are over, it seems an ideal time."

Oh, shit. He was coming after my job.

"Restructuring?"

"Everyone will have the opportunity to reapply for the jobs available. The new job descriptions will be out in the next few days. If people choose not to apply, they'll be paid out for their notice period, and be free to find work elsewhere. Do you have any questions?"

It all came at me fast, and I paused for a moment to think about what he'd said.

"Where's Kyle?" I asked.

That shook him. He stared at me for a moment before finally coming out with the words. "My son is on indefinite leave."

"But where is he? I need to talk to him."

"Rowan, he's not coming back. I think we both know why."

I was breathing fast now, fighting back the tears. "I didn't do anything. I just want to talk to him."

"I'm sorry, I can't talk to you about this any more. Please think about what I said, and if you do wish to reapply, let my assistant know."

Somehow I just knew there would only be one job cut. I wouldn't give him the satisfaction of turning me down.

"No. I don't wish to reapply because you will shut me out. I'm not stupid, Mr Warner; that's why I got the job in the first place."

He leaned back in his chair, clasping his hands together in some big grandiose gesture that I assumed was supposed to look intimidating.

"I'm insulted that you think I would put your whatever-it-was with my son over my business. Don't think for a moment that you have that much influence, young lady."

I didn't even stop to say goodbye, turning on my heel and walking out. I slammed the door hard behind me, and Miriam jumped as I walked past. There was a good chance I could seek legal advice, but why would I want to? Why would I want to stay where I wasn't wanted?

Behind me, his office door opened, but I wasn't turning back even to see if he was watching. Screw him, and screw his son. I had known the risks of getting involved with the boss's son, and the worst possible thing had happened.

I was in love with another man who didn't want me. The story of my life.

As I entered my office, I kicked the bin, and it clattered against the wall. To hell with this place. More than anything right now I wanted to be home with my mother, nursing my broken heart. The idea of finding another job to support myself was so far off I couldn't even think that way.

It wasn't like I had that much stuff. I could pack up and be out in the next few days.

I didn't want to run away, but how could I stay? In my head I could hear Andrew. "You're so anal, Rowan. Planning everything to the nth degree. No-one could ever accuse you of being spontaneous."

All my life I had loved him, put my life on hold, waiting for him to tell me he felt the same. Now all of it meant nothing as the man I truly loved thought I was a cheat, and a liar.

What a mess.

***

THE HEAVY RAIN outside woke me up. It lashed at the window as if it wanted in, and I watched as the drains overflowed, and the cars kept on going without a care, drenching the people on the footpath. *People suck.*

In less than fifteen minutes, I had packed my office up and left. I'd rather leave than have the indignity of being pushed out. For now,

I'd had enough of being humiliated. Andrew had done that often enough without me realising he was doing it.

There was a gentle tap on the door, and I ran, just in case it was Kyle. Andrew stood in the doorway, shivering and dripping water all over the floor.

"What do you want?" I asked.

"I came to see if you were okay. You know, after the other day. What an asshole, running out on you like that."

I turned back into the apartment, and he followed, taking off his coat and throwing it over the back of a chair. Water dripped on the chair, and I picked his coat up, growling at him as I took it over to the door where the lino would be much easier to wipe.

"He's not an asshole."

"Where is he now then, Rowan?"

I flopped onto the couch, lying down so he had to sit elsewhere.

"Row, please. You don't belong with him. If he cared he would have stopped to find out what was going on."

"Fuck you, Andrew. If you hadn't pulled that shit in the first place, none of this would have happened."

He leaned forward in his chair, and I felt uncomfortable under his gaze for the first time. "We were meant to be together. That's all there is to it. Charlie was an amazing woman, but it was always you, Row."

I jumped off the couch, feeling the anger grow as I crossed the room. My hand stung as I slapped his face, but I would have done it again in a heartbeat, he pissed me off that much.

"Don't you dare. I'm not the backup girlfriend. You're the asshole, Andrew. Thanks to you, I have lost the only man who has ever truly loved me for me. Not because I'm the substitute for the one you chose."

He shook his head. "That's not fair. You know I always cared about you. You were the first girl I kissed; the first one who let me touch her boob." He grinned, as if it were some big joke.

"If Charlie had been there instead of me, would you have felt her up instead?"

The grin disappeared from his face. It didn't take a genius to work out I'd got that right. "What are you going to do now, then?" he asked.

I shrugged. "Well, my job is basically gone, so I'm packing up to go home. I'll pick apples for the season, save some money, and think about what to do next."

"You're running away."

"If you want to see it that way. I can't breathe here. Not in the city where I found and lost the man I love. All I want to do is go home to my mother and be with people who love me."

He just looked at me, and I wanted so much to slap him again, but I couldn't bring myself to do it. "Charlie's been dead for only a few weeks, and you're talking about moving on with me. How is that right? It's disgusting that you taint the memory of her by trying this shit."

"She would have understood."

I shook my head. "No, she wouldn't. I wonder if you really knew her at all."

He stood, and there was this uncomfortable silence while I pretended he wasn't there anymore and he worked out what to say next.

"Just go, Andrew. Find someone else to screw and use, but not me."

For just a moment I thought he might try to rescue the situation. Say something meaningful. Instead he left in a huff, grabbing his coat on the way out and turning back towards me at the door.

"Do you know why I chose Charlie?"

I shook my head. "I don't want to know."

"She was gorgeous. All tits and legs, and I wanted to fuck her so badly I told her that I loved her. You just didn't compare, Rowan. You're smart and funny, but I wanted perfection."

I shook my head. "You know, not so long ago you saying that would have devastated me. Now it means nothing. I know you want to hurt me, and maybe you do think that way, but, Kyle loved me for me, and I'll get him back somehow. What I need right now is for you to get the hell out of my life. I don't ever want to see you again, and I hope you go to hell for the way you've treated your wife. She's not even cold, and all you want is someone to keep your bed warm. Selfish asshole."

He slammed the door when he left, and I felt nothing. The pain I'd been through finding out that he didn't love me was gone. Even his pathetic insults washed off me as if they were nothing. I took a deep breath, closing my eyes as a new wave of emotions washed over me. I'd never been so miserable as I was without Kyle, and yet I felt liberated more than ever. Spewing my distaste for Andrew at him was therapeutic, and I smiled at the thought of being free of him.

Now I had to make the effort to kick-start my life. Without Andrew, and with or without Kyle.

TWENTY-THREE

ROWAN

COMING HOME WAS BITTERSWEET. As much as I loved my parents, and the orchard, I felt like a complete and utter failure. Falling in love with the boss's son had ruined my great start to a career. Maybe I should have just stayed friends; that way I wouldn't have hurt him. Oh, who was I kidding? He loved me, he would have been hurt regardless.

I drove down the long driveway that cut through the centre of the orchard, towards the house. Dad was talking to someone, and my stomach dropped when I saw who it was. David, the guy who had hurt me all those years ago, was back working for him. He smiled and waved at me as I got out the car.

"Rowan? What are you doing here?" Dad asked, moving towards me and catching me as I fell into his arms. I didn't want to cry while David stood there watching, but I couldn't help it.

"Kyle left me," I whispered, feeling myself shake.

"It looks like everything you own is in the car," he said in disbelief. "What happened to your apartment?"

"I can't stay, Dad. Everything is a mess."

He hugged me tight, patting me on the back. "Go inside and see your mother. I'll be in shortly and we'll talk."

"How are you, Rowan?" David asked as I passed him on the way to the front door. I ignored him, twisting the door handle and stumbling through the doorway. My crappy day had just gotten even worse.

"Mum," I called, walking down the corridor that led to the kitchen at the back of the house. She stood there, ironing Dad's clothes. I never understood why she did that; he worked outside all of the time. Creases didn't matter, but they did to her. In a random moment of clarity, I suddenly understood where some of my eccentricities came from.

"Rowan? Oh, love, it's so good to see you." She stepped around the ironing board, holding me tight as I burst into tears in her arms.

"What's wrong, love?" She looked at me, her eyes sad as if she felt what I was feeling.

"Everything is just so screwed up." I sniffed. I heard Dad come in behind me, and sit at the dining table.

"What's going on, sweetheart? We love seeing you, but not this way," he said.

"Kyle left me. His dad implied that I was going to lose my job, so I packed up and left."

His face dropped. "We can do something about that if it's related to you and Kyle breaking up."

I shook my head. "I told him what I think. That's enough for me."

"You're too kind-hearted," Mum said, "I agree with Dad."

I growled, taking a seat next to Dad at the table. Mum sat opposite, looking at me like a wounded child.

"What happened with Kyle? He seemed like such a nice boy."

"It was Andrew's fault."

At that, they looked at each other.

"What?" I asked.

"Rowan, this whole thing with Andrew. It's gone on for far too long." Dad said.

"It wasn't my fault. He came over all upset about Charlie, and I tried to help him. He made it look like we had slept together, and Kyle got the wrong idea. I can't talk to him; he's gone underground rather than speaking with me about it."

Dad put his hand on my shoulder. "It's okay, love. I wasn't blaming you. It's just that you were hung up on that boy for so many years, and he wasn't worthy of you. He's a sneaky little bastard. I don't know if you remember, but he used to get you in trouble quite often when you were younger."

I shook my head. "I don't remember that. Though, while we're on the topic of sneaky bastards, why do you have David working for you again?"

Guilt crossed his face. "I had trouble finding workers for the season. He showed up and had the experience. I'm sorry, Rowan. It was a few years ago, and he's got a wife and kid now. I thought I'd help him out for the season and with you not living here, I didn't think you would run into him."

"So now who's too kind-hearted?" I said, cocking an eyebrow.

He smirked. "I know. I think you have your father to blame for that trait. We can work something out. Maybe you could find a job around here, or help your mother out while you work through this. You don't have to be out in the orchard."

I shook my head. "It's okay, Dad. I'll do whatever I have to. I'm not the same person I was four years ago either."

He smiled. "I can see that. I've always been so proud of you, sweetheart."

BEING BACK in my room was weird. The last time I was there was the wedding, when Kyle had told me he loved me, turning my knees to jelly when he'd kissed me. He was so sure of himself, and for the first time I'd felt as if someone was really being honest with their feelings toward me. Everything was ruined now.

Andrew. It all came back to him. My unrequited love; my ruin. I'd loved him my whole life, and now I regretted ever meeting him. My heart was still broken over Charlie's death. They'd both kept their relationship a secret from me, but she was the one who had voiced her regret over it. Not Andrew. I don't think he even cared.

I wish I knew where you were.

Checking my phone for the millionth time, just in case Kyle had messaged me, left me feeling empty. There was nothing but all the text messages I'd sent him.

I unpacked the car into a space my dad made me in the shed near the house, bursting into tears at the sight of that damn console. Kyle had bought that to apologise, but now I saw it was his way of getting to know me. I'd been so blind to his intentions, and now I had nothing of him, not even his friendship.

After dinner, I crawled into bed to feel sorry for myself. Mum tapped on the door, entering with a cup of cocoa in her hand. "Here you go, love. Just like you used to have it."

I sat up, clutching the mug to me. "Thanks, Mum."

She sat on the bed, stroking my leg. "You okay??"

I shook my head. "I love Kyle. I hate this."

Her brows furrowed. "What was Andrew thinking? That poor girl has only been gone a short time, and he's causing trouble for you?"

"I know. I told him he was disgusting."

Tears rolled down my cheeks, and Mum frowned. "I'm so sorry to hear it. Tell you what, though, I truly believe that if you're meant to be with Kyle, you'll find a way back to one another."

"I hope so," I whispered.

"Did I ever tell you the story of how I ended up with your father?" she asked, a wistful smile spreading across her face.

"No. Didn't you two go to school together or something?"

"We did. We were friends, but not close friends. I had a thing for your uncle, Alan."

I nearly spat the cocoa out over the bed. "You had a thing for Dad's brother?"

"He was older, and he had a car of his own. I was star struck, though. I knew your Dad had a crush on me. He was so sweet, but Alan was exciting. Then, Alan asked me out."

"Did you go out with him?"

She nodded. "Honey, it was as boring as watching paint dry. All he talked about was himself. We saw a movie, and he drove me home, stopping outside the house and unzipping his pants."

I knew I was gaping, but I couldn't help it. My mother never talked about sex. It had been Dad who talked to us girls about the birds and the bees, and even then the discussion was mostly thrusting a book about it at us and telling us we could go to him if we needed any more information. Of course, none of us ever did.

"You and Uncle Alan?"

She shook her head. "He indicated that he wanted me to ..." She looked around as if she thought she was being watched.

"Go down on him?"

"I guess that's what it's called."

"So Uncle Alan wanted a blow job. And you said what?"

"I told him no. That I wasn't that kind of girl. He told me to get out of the car."

I smiled at her. My mother was quiet, like me, and I was so proud that she'd stood up for herself.

"I was upset at how everything had ended, and went around the back of the house so I could sneak in and not have my mother see. Your father was sitting on the doorstep. I don't know how long he'd been there, but he had a handful of apple blossoms that he'd picked for me. He knew, Rowan. He knew what his brother was like and he waited to pick up the pieces, because he knew I wouldn't like what I saw. We were just meant to be, and we still are perfect for each other. You and your sisters are testament to that."

I sniffed, wiping my eyes with the blanket.

"So you see, Rowan, if Kyle is the right one for you, you'll find a way. Maybe one day he'll be sitting on the doorstep with apple blossoms in his hand, maybe he'll pick up the phone and call you when he's ready. Whatever happens, he's an idiot for walking away from my perfect girl, but I think he'll work that out soon enough."

She stood, bending over to kiss my cheek. "Don't settle for anything less than perfect. You deserve that much."

I watched as she left the room, pausing at the door to wink at me before leaving. Looking down at my cocoa, I sighed. I'd have given anything to be with Kyle right this minute. In his arms, in his bed ... But I couldn't push him. He had to work it out for himself.

TWENTY-FOUR

ROWAN

DOWN A ROW, picking apples, I heard a low wolf whistle behind me. Rolling my eyes, I stepped down off the ladder to find David walking towards me, a stupid grin on his face. I'd managed to avoid him for the first week, the orchard big enough for me to tuck myself away. My luck had run out.

"Looking good, Rowan. How have you been? First time you've stood still long enough for me to talk to you." His blue eyes twinkled, as if we were friends or something.

"I'm fine. And busy." I turned back towards the tree.

"Didn't expect to see you back here. I thought you'd got all high and mighty and found a real job."

"Yeah I did, but I'm back for a short time."

"How come?"

I turned back towards him. "Not really any of your business. I just want to help my dad out."

"He had real trouble finding workers this year. I think he's really struggling."

"It's always up and down. He'll be fine. Now, if you don't mind, I'd like to get on with what I'm doing, as I'm really close to finishing."

He took a step closer, and I swallowed hard, uncomfortable in his presence.

"We never got to finish, sweetheart. Maybe you'd like to revisit that this time around?"

"That would be a no. Dad said you were married, anyway."

He grinned that charming grin that had gotten me into trouble so many years ago. "So you asked about me?"

"Uh, no. I was surprised Dad hired you again, that's all. I don't care what you've done with your life."

"Whatever." He leaned forward. "I still remember you on your knees with your lips wrapped around my ..."

"Rowan." Dad was calling from another row. He was out of sight, but maybe his Dad radar was going.

"I'm over here, Dad," I called back, smiling at David.

"Lucky," David whispered. "I was about to ask for a repeat performance."

"Well, let's just say that unless you learn to suck it for yourself, no one around here will be doing it." I grinned, and moved around him towards my father, who was looking at me curiously. David stared at me open-mouthed. I would never have said anything like that to him the last time we saw one another, but then, I wasn't that girl anymore.

"Everything all right here?" Dad asked.

"Everything's fine," I said.

He put his arm around my waist. "Your mother is cooking a pork roast for dinner tonight, and I reminded her that you knew how to get the crackling just perfect. Do you want to go in early?"

"Sure." I pecked him on the cheek. That was as good excuse as any to get me out of this situation.

He eyed up David and grabbed my arm, leading me back to the house.

"Was he being difficult?" he asked, when we were a distance away.

"A little. Nothing I couldn't handle."

He frowned. "If it does bother you, I'll get rid of him."

"Don't worry about it, Dad. Get the season's work out of him. You need the staff. I'm not going to interfere with that. It can't be that hard to stay away from him. I think he got the message."

TWENTY-FIVE

ROWAN

DAVID HAD STAYED AWAY from me since the day I slapped him down, and he looked terrified when I smiled sweetly at his wife when she brought him his lunch one day.

The satisfaction that I got out of that moment was the only solace I had in what was one of the most difficult times of my life. As the days ticked by, being reunited with Kyle grew less likely, and after trying to reach out to him for three weeks I realised I needed to come to terms with it being over.

For such a short time, I had known what it was to be loved. To find perfection in a world surrounded by lies and deception, uncertainty and fear. Now, the only man to ever truly love me was gone, no calls returned, not a word from him.

I knew he was acting childish, that he should have stayed and talked to me, but I understood why he freaked out, knowing everything he did about my past, and my feelings for Andrew.

I just really missed him.

Dad kept me busy. It had been a bumper crop, and he was going to do well this year. I was glad that I could help. There were so many memories tied to this place, though, not just of Dad, but of Andrew.

In many ways this was the best and the worst place I could have come.

There were only a few days left of picking, and I looked at the tree in front of me, sighing at the thought of having to find another job. None of this was fair.

Slowly, I climbed the ladder. Somewhere in the distance I heard a wolf whistle. I ignored it, climbing the rest of the way until I was at the right height to pick the apples.

Someone grabbed my leg a few minutes later and I squealed, turning around to see who I was about to kick. "I told you to leave me alone, you dirty ..." I swear to God that my heart stopped. It was Kyle.

"You haven't seen me in a while, and you're calling me names?"

"I ... It's complicated. I didn't know it was you."

"Well, surprise." He grinned that perfect grin that made my heart ache. I wanted more than anything for him to just kiss me.

"What are you doing here? After you walked out and ignored me, I didn't think I'd ever see you again."

Now he looked sheepish. "I was pretty childish. It hurt seeing you with Andrew when I thought we had a thing."

"It wasn't what it looked like." I came back down the ladder and stood facing him. Despite everything, all I wanted was for him to take me in his arms and love me. The whole job thing didn't matter. I'd work in the orchard forever if it meant he was part of my life.

I'd dithered for so long, not realising he felt the same way I did. Now, all I wanted to know was why he was here, and if this meant we had a chance. All these thoughts ran through my head, but I couldn't find the words to speak. If I did, I'd start crying, and telling him how much I'd missed him.

He wasn't helping. He just stood there, and looked back at me. An eternity passed as we stood in silence.

"Rowan, I ..."

"What are you doing here, Kyle? I thought that you were well and truly finished with me after I basically lost my job."

He put his hand to his heart, the one I hoped still belonged to me.

"I had no idea that had happened. After that day at your apartment, I left town for a while. I ignored your messages, that much is true. It hurt too much to think about it all. When I came back, I found out what Dad had done. I'm so sorry."

I looked over his shoulder, too afraid to meet his eye. Regardless of that, I could feel the tears building after I'd been sure I'd cried all the tears I had over him.

"I came after you that day, you know. When it sunk in what had happened, I ran out, but you were already gone. I was such a mess."

He took a step towards me. "I understand. It caught me by surprise. Here we were, ready to move on with our relationship, and next thing, I think you're with Andrew. It threw me, Rowan and I screwed up big time, not knowing how to handle it."

I took a deep breath. Was this really it? Either he was here to tell me to my face that it was over, or he wanted me back. It sounded like the latter; I hoped more than anything it was the latter.

"If you're going to put me out of my misery, just do it," I whispered, choking back the tears.

"I love you, Rowan. That's all there is to it. Can you forgive me? If I'd been there, I would have stopped Dad from that stupid restructuring. He did it for me, thinking it would be what I wanted, but nothing could have been further from the truth. All it did was give Ross what he wanted, and to hell with him."

Gasping for air, I let go of the tears as the words sunk in.

"Rowan. Please?" He moved closer. I could smell his aftershave now, that subtle, sexy smell I had come to love. He loved me, despite me keeping him at arm's length for all that time.

"I love you too. I was so stupid, holding onto the past for so long when what I needed was right in front of me. I'm the one who's sorry."

Before I could take another breath I was in his arms, and he kissed my tears away before he kissed my lips. He was so loving and tender, I began to cry all over again.

"Stop crying, baby," he said.

"I thought ... I thought I'd lost you."

Kyle picked me up off the ground, spinning me around until I laughed. "Never," he said, kissing me again and again.

He smelt so good and I clung to him, terrified it would all turn out to be a dream.

"Rowan, I'm not going anywhere. I swear."

I closed my eyes, feeling his strong arms around me. These past weeks I'd tortured myself not knowing if I would ever see him again. Now everything was as it should be.

"Is everything all right, Rowan?" My father's voice came from behind me.

I turned towards him, my arms still tight around Kyle, and I nodded. "Things are fine, Dad."

Kyle stiffened, and I felt it as he extended his hand. "Mr Taylor."

Dad nodded, and I could see his uncertainty at shaking Kyle's hand. This was, after all, the man I'd been crying over the past few weeks.

"Kyle and I are sorting things out. Everything is good now." I smiled at him. I must have lit up like a Christmas tree, as my father's expression showed he understood completely.

"That's good. Come up to the house, and we'll have a coffee. Rowan's mother has made a cake, if I'm not mistaken, from the smell."

"That would be great, Sir," Kyle said.

We watched my father walk away. I looked up at Kyle. He had the same silly grin on his face I was sure I had.

"You know, Rowan, one day I'm going to marry you among the apple trees," he said.

I laughed. "It's too soon to be talking marriage. We've only just become a real couple."

He nodded. "I know. Just making my intention clear. It's so beautiful here. All I want to do now is to carry you home and go to bed."

"If you're staying here, it'll be a celibate night. We were lucky we got away with so much last time without a stink."

He looked at me in mock horror. "What? You mean I have to wait?"

"Well, maybe I could sneak down the hall. I'm assuming you're not running back home tonight."

"I don't want to go without you. If I go back, I want you with me. Otherwise, I guess I have a new career picking apples."

I squeezed his hand, laughing. "Kyle, I love that you feel that way, but I need to sort myself out, save some money before I can go back. I need to find a job."

"Your old job is waiting for you. It didn't really go anywhere. You can stay with me, or find somewhere by yourself nearby. I'll help you."

I took him by the hand, leading him towards the house. David was skulking in the trees as we drew closer, and I saw him raise an eyebrow at Kyle.

I grinned, wrapping my arm around Kyle's waist. He stopped walking for a moment, pulling me in for a kiss.

"Are we going to get to the house?" he asked when I let him go.

"Dad will send out a search party if we don't."

He stroked my face with the palm of his hand. "Wouldn't want that to happen." I felt him run his hand down my back as he had at the wedding. "I love you, Rowan, and I'm never going to stop telling you."

"How did you work out the truth?"

He grimaced. "I went home yesterday, and went out for a drink last night. I wanted to forget, and coming home just made me think about you. I ran into Andrew at a bar with some girl. When I told him I was surprised he wasn't there with you, he told me that you'd kicked him out. He was really drunk so told me quite a lot. I got the whole story."

I buried my face in his chest, breathing in his scent. It felt so good just to be together again. I wasn't planning on letting him go any time soon.

"I listened to all your messages. I'm sorry for hurting you so much. I guess we both need to work out how to have a real relation-ship. Missed you," he whispered into my hair.

"You too." I tilted my face to be kissed again. There would have to be a lot of kisses to make up for our separation, but I was sure Kyle would oblige.

TWENTY-SIX

ROWAN

THE DOOR CREAKED as I pushed it open, and I closed my eyes, thinking for some reason this would stop Mum and Dad hearing. Kyle sat on the side of the bed in just boxer shorts, and looked surprised as I padded across the carpet in bare feet.

"What are you doing here?"

I slid the straps of my nightgown down my arms, letting it fall to the floor. His jaw dropped as he looked over my body, his breathing growing heavier.

"Rowan," he whispered.

I walked to the side of the bed, bending to kiss him. He slid his hands down my back, stroking the tops of my thighs as he pulled me closer.

"You're not wearing any underwear."

I grinned. "I didn't see the point."

"Is this really what you want?"

I nodded, chewing my bottom lip. "At least we have more room in this bed."

He laughed, and pulled me closer, teasing my nipples with his tongue one by one. "The thought of these drove me crazy," he said. He sucked my nipple into his mouth, probing between my legs with his fingers.

"Kyle," I whispered.

"Get in this bed, now. You won't be leaving it tonight."

"I thought you didn't want to have sex under my parents' roof?" I teased.

"I'm over waiting. We'll just have to be quiet, and if we get caught, I'm pretty sure I can outrun your father."

I laughed, climbing over him and into the bed.

Reaching into his overnight bag, he pulled out a box of condoms. "I think we might need all of these."

I laughed. "All of them?"

"You have no idea how many times I've thought about this. How many times you have left me with the biggest erection I've ever had. Seriously, I could have stabbed things some nights."

I covered my mouth, giggling as he leaned over to kiss me.

"I love you. Nothing is going to come between us now," he said.

I nodded and he nestled beside me, taking me in his arms to kiss me. "Do you remember what I told you about those freckles of yours?"

"Yes," I whispered.

"I'm starting my exploration tonight. It might take me some time."

"Take as long as you need."

He reached between my legs, sliding his fingers between my folds, stroking my clit. "I'm sure there are plenty down here. I might have to thoroughly investigate with my tongue."

A shiver went through me. I'd never had anyone go down on me, and the thought of it made me moan with desire.

"I want to be your first for everything, Rowan. First and last."

I nodded, and he kissed me before going back to work on my nipples. They were hard with anticipation, and sensitive to his tongue. His strokes grew faster as he sucked and lapped, and my body grew warm as my climax approached.

"Kyle."

He stopped what he was doing long enough to look at me.

"Yes?"

"I'm glad it's you. It feels so good."

He grinned. "You ain't seen nothing yet, baby."

I could feel my body giving in to him, could smell my scent as his fingers continued their work. "Kyle," I whispered more urgently.

"Let it go, Rowan."

His lips were on mine as I cried out his name, trying to stop me from making too much noise. My muscles contracted as I came, each wave hitting me harder than the last. I shuddered, and he moved his face between my legs, his hot breath on my sex nearly sending me over the top again.

He rolled his tongue over my clit, still so sensitive from his fingers. He stroked my breasts as he tongued me, pinching my nipples as I grew close to coming again. This time I didn't make a noise, gasping for breath as my body shook.

"You're so wet, baby," he said, reaching for the condom box. "Are you really ready?"

I nodded, unable to form words. Watching as he rolled the condom on, I wanted to touch him so much. He leaned over me, and I ran my hand up his chest. "I want to make you feel that good," I whispered.

"You will. There's plenty of time for that."

I could feel his tip at my entrance. "Last chance. Is this what you want?" he asked.

"There's nothing I want more right now."

He grinned, slowly pushing into me. I gasped again at the brief discomfort before closing my eyes as he pushed all the way in. "Rowan, look at me."

I opened my eyes. Every emotion he was feeling showed in his expression. "I love you so much," he said.

He began to move, and with every stroke the discomfort lessened, and I was left with the feeling of him filling me. I wanted him so deep inside me we'd become one, and I moved my hips to meet him, driving him in as far as he could get.

"Holy shit, Rowan."

"I missed you so much. Don't ever leave me again."

He shook his head. "Never, baby. You'll never get rid of me now."

I laughed and he leaned over to kiss me. "I love you more than anything. Nothing is going to keep me from you."

He bent his head to suck at my nipples again. I'd been so self-conscious even as I'd stripped off my nightgown, but that seemed to disappear as I gave him every part of me. He liked my breasts, even if I hated them. He loved all those things I hated about myself. This was perfect; he was perfect.

I felt him tense as he moved faster, hammering into me as if he were driving it home that he was inside. "Oh God," he said.

I smiled at the look on his face. He was floating somewhere; I had done that to him. He fell back to earth as he groaned in my ear, slowly pulling out of me and rolling to my side.

"That was amazing." He kissed me tenderly, nuzzling my nose with his own.

"For me too."

"I hope it didn't hurt too much."

I shook my head. "It was wonderful. You're wonderful."

He rolled off the bed, pulling on his boxers. "Where are you going?"

"To the bathroom. I need to get rid of this." He held up the condom.

"Grab a bin liner from the cupboard. We'll throw them all out in the morning discreetly, rather than flush them. Knowing my luck, it'll get stuck if you flush," I said.

Kyle laughed. "Always practical. I'm impressed you said *them*. Do you really want to see if we can finish the box?"

"I don't know about that, but I think we could make a dent." I grinned.

Lying back in the bed while he left the room, I was sure my body glowed from the love we had just shared. I felt warm, wanted, loved—everything I ever wanted to feel.

TWENTY-SEVEN

ROWAN

MOVING in with Kyle was the easy part; going back to work was tricky.

On my first day, Kyle's dad greeted me , and he asked me to go to his office. Kyle had wanted to come in with me, but this was my conversation to have.

He sat at his desk, smiling nervously as I sat opposite.

"Rowan, I'm glad you're back. Your job is as it was, and your office. I'm truly sorry for what happened. Kyle tells me that you are together, and I am happy for you both. He was just so wrecked by his last relationship, and I wanted to protect him. I went the wrong way about it, and I hope you can forgive me."

I sighed, shrugging. "I love Kyle, Mr Warner, and I want to make him happy and be happy." I chewed my bottom lip as I summoned up the courage for the next words. "Kyle told me my job was here, but I don't know if I can come back. Maybe I need to find something else."

He shook his head. "No way. We need you, Rowan. This whole new system is turning out to be a real nightmare, and it is really clear to me now that Ross can't handle it by himself. While you were working on your project, you got to know it better than anyone."

"I didn't screw up. You know that now, don't you?"

He nodded. "It became more and more obvious after you left." He grinned. "Welcome to the family, Rowan. I'm glad you're back, and not just because of this place. I've never seen Kyle so empty, so deflated, than he was without you. If he hadn't found out the truth, he might well have taken off overseas again."

We left his office, and he walked me through to mine. Ross was walking in the opposite direction, and stopped when he saw me.

"Rowan?"

"Rowan's coming back to work. She'll be taking back over the new system and iron out any bugs," Mr Warner said.

"I see," Ross said. He was suddenly a spectacularly pale shade as the colour drained from his face. That he hadn't been told this was happening filled me with joy. This was better than any revenge plot I could have thought up.

I sat down and started work. The system was a mess. It would take some time to go through and tidy things up, but it would keep me busy, and soon I would get it running smoothly.

My favourite part of the whole day was going home with Kyle. We went back to his apartment, and cooked dinner together, before curling up on the couch to play games.

The console had brought us together, and now we laughed and loved our way through the evening. Nothing felt better than snuggling up in bed at night with him. Every night was an adventure as I caught up on all those years I'd wanted to be loved.

The feeling of knowing where I stood with him was indescribable. There was never any doubt between the two of us, and our friendship had helped us form this deep, loving relationship. For the first time in my adult life, I was truly happy.

He was my best friend, my lover, and all of a sudden, my organised life was turned upside down by a man who made me feel more free than ever before.

There were times when we met up with his old friends. They were understandably cautious after what he'd been through with his last girlfriend, but they soon warmed to me when they realised I was nothing like her.

Before Kyle, my life had been lonely and quiet. Now it was filled with fun and noise, and chaos. And I loved every minute of it.

Whatever we did, I spent every night in Kyle's arms, feeling wanted and loved. I couldn't imagine being any happier.

I STILL HEARD from Andrew from time to time, the odd email, or text message, always apologetic about what happened, always reassuring me that he missed my friendship and that was it. Kyle knew about it all, just as he knew about my decision to keep Andrew at arm's length.

It wouldn't be fair to Kyle after everything that had happened to renew my friendship with Andrew. And it wasn't fair for Andrew to think that I wanted the closeness we had once shared. Although as time went on, I realised that it was a long time since we'd actually had that closeness as opposed to how I had once perceived things.

I'd never had so much clarity in my whole life. Kyle's love had brought that to me because now I knew what it was like to really mean something to someone.

And it felt wonderful.

TWENTY-EIGHT

KYLE

EVERY DAY she grew in confidence. Being loved and knowing it did wonders for Rowan's self-esteem, and it flowed through to every aspect of her life, including work.

She'd already had that confidence in her skills, now it flowed through to her behaviour, and it made me so proud to see her sticking up for herself. Ross never stood a chance once she was back.

Dad was delighted when she came up with new ideas for all the computer systems, without the need for him to spend huge amounts of money. When she got the green light for those ideas, she glowed with excitement. Now, she not only got to prove that she knew what she was talking about, but she got a certain amount of payback for being stitched up before.

And then I got to go home with her.

She was still reticent at times, but bolder and more decisive. The shyness showed through when she was being flirtatious, looking out at me under those eyelashes. She made my stomach do flips and all I could think about was possessing her.

I loved her more and more each day, and best of all? No crazy stuff. We'd both found what we were looking for in each other.

My friends, who had been driven away by my ex's antics, had begun to renew their friendships with me. Rowan's gentle ways soon won them over, and she suddenly had her pick of friends to choose from. Surrounded by people who adored her, she thrived, and the world became so much bigger than the tiny bubble she'd created around herself. And yet, if they all disappeared tomorrow, and it was just the two of us again, we'd cope fine.

SHE LAY ON THE BED, sucking on her fingers, keeping eye contact as I stripped off. I went straight in, my head between her legs, giving her what we both needed: my tongue inside her, probing her wetness as she relaxed and sighed, giving in to the demands I placed on her body. As I flicked my tongue over her clit, gently sucking on it, she bucked her hips, moaning, gripping my hair, and pulling me in to her climax.

I moved over her, kissing her lips and meeting her tongue as she kissed me. Where she was once shy and tentative, we now did battle for supremacy, for ownership, and I gave in to her. *Always.*

She pushed me, flipping me onto my back and rocking her groin against mine. Once again, she had me just where she wanted me, and there was nowhere else I wanted to be. "Rowan," I said, running my hands from her neck down her breasts, and pulling her up to my torso so I could slide my fingers into her.

Rowan leaned back, giving me better access as I rubbed her clit with my thumb. She shuddered, rolling off me and moving beside to go down on me, taking me in her mouth and lovingly running her tongue down my length. Grinning as she came back up, she bit down on her lip rather than keep going. What a tease. "I love it when you do that," I said, stroking her hair. She was in full command, whether she realised it or not.

She sat up, grabbing the box on the bedside cabinet and taking a condom from it, rolled it down my cock as I watched her. She frowned as she sat astride me, lowering herself slowly. I filled her and she leaned forward to kiss me.

"You don't have to look unhappy about it." I laughed. I knew why she was looked that way, but in a few moments, I'd get that smile back on her face.

I pulled her over, flipping her onto her back this time, and she smiled, her eyes warm with the love she felt for me. When our eyes met, and I saw that look, I knew I was home.

"I just …" Her sentence went unfinished as I pulled back and thrust hard into her. Distracted, she moaned, meeting my hips for the second thrust, her body possessed by our joining together, and I knew I had her.

Our lovemaking had become more energetic as the confidence she had in her body grew. I worshipped every inch of her, and once she'd accepted that as fact and not as me trying to make her feel better about some imagined flaw, she'd become bolder in bed. It was amazing; she was amazing.

I pinned her to the bed, holding her arms as I pounded into her, deeper and deeper as she thrust back. I let go with a groan, crashing my lips into hers with another kiss that consumed us both. She hooked her legs around mine, not letting me pull out, and I laughed, rubbing my nose to hers and planting tiny kisses on her face.

"Got you," she whispered.

"Always." She let me go so I could roll to the side, panting at the effort.

I reached for her, pulling her face towards me to keep kissing her. "I love you," she said. Not that she needed to; it was written all over her face.

"I love you too." I ran a finger down between her breasts, and she wriggled over to snuggle.

"Hang on, gotta go sort this out." I climbed out of bed, pulling the condom off. When I came back, she was frowning again.

"I hate having to stop for those things." She pouted, and I kissed her nose.

"I know." She had tried going on the pill, but had a bad reaction to it. Back to the drawing board we'd gone, so we were using the rubber interrupters, as I liked to call them. "Rowan, we'll work it out. If this is all we have to worry about, we don't have that many issues."

I climbed back in to bed beside her, and pulled her into my arms for a kiss. "As long as we're together, none of the other shit matters. It'll do for now. Thank fuck you're not allergic to latex."

She laughed, pinching my butt.

I sighed. "Look, if you're going to sexually harass me, I'll have no choice but to have sex with you again."

"What a shame," she said straight-faced, pinching me once more.

"You're just asking for trouble, aren't you?"

"Maybe." She poked her tongue at me, and I grabbed it between my teeth, wiggling my eyebrows as she laughed. I let go, shaking my head.

"I'm just a sex object to you, Rowan. That's all I am."

"Oh, woe is you." She rolled over onto her side. "Look, I'm facing away so I don't objectify you."

I reached over her, pulling her against me, rubbing my already hardening cock between her legs. "You know I love it when you use big words." I sucked on her earlobe, fondling a breast, and she giggled as she pushed back against me.

"So, forgetting the slight disruption, are you ready for round two?" I whispered in her ear, my fingers probing her and finding the answer without her using words.

I'd never thought I'd find someone so perfectly suited to me, but Rowan and I, we were destined to spend our lives together. If I was ever sure of anything, that was it, and she felt the same way.

Two hours later, we sat, naked and cross-legged in the middle of the living room floor. Rowan had challenged me to a race, and I was trying my best to keep up as our cars zoomed around the track on screen.

I didn't care if I lost; the sight of her relaxed and enjoying herself brought me more joy than I would ever admit to. We laughed and loved, revelling in the blissful serenity of our relationship.

There was one thing that I was certain about. I was going to marry this girl, make her mine until the end of time. And I was sure she loved that idea too.

TWENTY-NINE

KYLE

I WATCHED her sleep as I climbed into bed beside her. She was so peaceful, her hair a mess from our earlier activities. All she'd ever needed was an outlet for the love she had to give, a partner to share with her rather than taking what they could and throwing her away. Now, she had me.

Taking her hand in mine, I looked at the ring in my other hand. Dad hadn't been surprised when I'd asked for it, even gave us his blessing, though that was never really a problem. He adored her too. This had been my mother's ring, and she had long, slender fingers just like Rowan. Most memories I'd had of Mum had faded, but I still remembered those fingers, stroking my cheek as she told me she was proud of me, and that Dad would take care of me now.

I fought back the tears that threatened as every piece of emotion that connected me to that memory came to the surface and smiling, I slid the ring onto Rowan's left ring finger. The thought of her waking up to find it there filled me with a warm buzz, and I closed my eyes, trying to let the good vibe take over the sadness that threatened to engulf me.

Over the years I'd thought about Mum often, but now more than ever, I wished she were here to meet Rowan. She'd love her too, I knew that for a fact.

I'd even called Rowan's father, and he was only too happy to give us his blessing too. Our parents all knew we were just meant to be.

The ring was a little loose, but would stay in place, and I placed Rowan's hand back under the blanket where it would be warm. In the morning I'd get her answer, but placing the ring on her finger was enough for now. I'd go to sleep a happy man, dreaming of our life together.

She woke me with kisses, her soft lips brushing across my face and giggled when I opened my eyes.

"Are you okay, Rowan?" I asked, trying hard to contain the grin that threatened to break out.

Holding up her hand, she pressed her lips to mine before breaking away and squealing again.

"You like it, then?" The diamond glistened in the morning light, and she squeezed me tight, clearly unable to verbalise how she was feeling.

"Rowan, talk to me." I laughed, nuzzling her cheek with my nose.

"It's beautiful," she finally said, almost whispering the words.

"Not as beautiful as you."

I hadn't made her blush in a while, but at that she did, her cheeks flushing with colour as she tried to bury her face in my chest.

"Don't believe you've given me an answer, Miss Taylor?" I already knew the answer from her reaction, but wanted to hear it from her lips.

She raised her face and smiled. "That depends on the question."

I laughed. "The rock on your finger isn't enough? Do you really want me to ask?"

Rowan planted a kiss on my chest. "Ask me the question, Warner," she whispered. She looked up at me, those beautiful eyes of her pulling me in.

"Will you marry me, Rowan?" I said, stroking her face with my fingers.

"You know I will," she whispered, pushing me back on the bed, rolling on top of me as if claiming me.

"So that's a yes, then?" I ran my fingers down her back, feeling her lips on mine as we got lost in one another again.

I could spend the rest of my life doing this with her, and I would never have anything to complain about.

"That's a yes," she whispered, pressing her nose to mine.

God, I love her.

THIRTY

ROWAN

KYLE KEPT his word about marrying me among the apple trees. In the spring, the orchard was covered in apple blossoms, and we planned our wedding surrounded by flowers. Despite everything, I couldn't help thinking about Charlie. Her asthma had meant she had never been allowed to visit me here, but I missed her being around for my wedding.

She hadn't deserved the treatment she'd had in death from Andrew. Any thought of him disgusted me now. He was a user and not worth thinking about, but of course I thought about them both today.

Kyle was loving, protective, and everything else I needed. I couldn't ask for a better man to be my husband.

His father had travelled down for the wedding, intending to stay at a nearby motel. He hit it off with my dad, opting instead to take up the offer to stay. Everyone I loved, everyone who was family, were all under the same roof.

I got an email the night before the wedding. Everyone had gone to bed, Kyle in the spare room for the last time, and I was glad I was alone when it arrived as it was from Andrew.

. . .

Hey Row,

I'm sorry for everything. Especially what I said to you when we argued. I didn't mean any of it; I just lashed out. You and Charlie meant the world to me, but things just worked out with her. I never saw you as a back-up or second best; I loved you both equally. No matter how hard I try, I can't forget either of you.

Whatever happens, I love you, Rowan. Now and forever. If you ever need me, you know where I am.

Good luck with Kyle. Tomorrow he'll be the luckiest man alive to marry you. I hope he realises that.

Love,
Andrew

I LOOKED AT THE SCREEN, tears rolling down my face. For all his words, to pull this on the eve of my wedding was manipulative and so low. Only now I could see it for what it was, and know it wasn't just some declaration of love. Even if he meant it, it didn't matter anymore. I smiled as I pressed delete.

Behind my door hung my wedding dress in the suit bag. Part of me wanted to take it out and try it on again, but knowing my luck I'd spill something all over it. I couldn't wait for Kyle to see me in it. I couldn't wait to share my secret with him. Just one night to go and I would be his wife, and he would know that his child was growing inside me.

For a week I'd been sitting on that. Keeping it a secret had been hard, but I couldn't imagine a better time to tell him than the day we exchanged wedding vows.

I snuggled down into my bed, smiling as I closed my eyes. One more sleep to go.

OUTSIDE, it was still dark when he crept into my room the morning of the wedding.

"What are you doing?" I whispered.

"Move over. I'm coming in for a cuddle."

I laughed as we squeezed into the bed together. "At least next time we stay with your parents they'll be okay with us sleeping together."

"You shouldn't be here. Isn't it bad luck for you to see me before the wedding?"

He grinned. "Are you wearing your dress? No. That's the bad luck part. It's not unlucky for me to see you naked before the wedding."

I could feel him pulling at the bottom of my nightgown. "Kyle, stop it. Just behave."

"That would be impossible around you." He kissed me, pulling my nightgown halfway up my back.

"You're naughty, Mr Warner."

"Just as naughty as you, Mrs Soon-To-Be Warner." He kissed me gently. "I love you, Rowan."

"I love you too."

"Do you remember the day we met?"

I laughed. "Of course I do. I rescued you from the rain."

He laughed.

"And then, we met again." I smiled as I said the words.

"All I remember is seeing that beautiful rear end, and I just wanted to slap it. Little did I know what an amazing woman I was about to nearly offend."

I buried my face in his chest, suffocating the laughter coming out of me.

"Somehow I resisted the urge, and found myself looking into the most beautiful eyes I'd ever seen. And then you categorised me as a friend and nothing more."

I knew I was gaping. "I did not."

"You totally did. It was all *Andrew this* and *Andrew that*. I never got a look in." He grinned. "I won in the end, though."

"I thought you were gorgeous, and I never thought I would stand a chance with someone like you. I think I did alright for myself." I nuzzled his cheek.

He kissed me, and I closed my eyes thinking about how lucky I was. He loved me, truly loved me. Nothing in the world could ever top this feeling. I thought of the tiny human growing inside me, and I wanted to tell him so badly. Somehow I stopped myself; that was news for later, my wedding gift to him.

"I don't want to leave this bed, but I think your mother might chase me out of the house if I don't go," he said.

"Just a little longer?"

I felt his arms around me, hugging me tight. "After tomorrow, nothing on this earth is keeping me from your bed. No matter how small it is."

He released me, kissing me on the nose to say goodbye. "You are my everything, Rowan. Never forget that."

I could feel the tears building as he climbed off the bed. "Kyle?"

"Yes, baby?"

I smiled at him. "See you soon?"

"Wouldn't miss it for the world."

He winked before taking a peep out the door to see if anyone was in the hallway. I lay back in bed, thinking about the day ahead. In a few hours, I would be his wife and we would start our new life together.

I dozed for a while longer, before Mum came in to wake me.

"I'm so proud of you, love," she said. "He's a good man. You found someone who will love and take care of you. I couldn't ask for more."

"He really does love me, Mum. I love him so much too. He's the most amazing person I think I've ever met."

"So, no more moping around about Andrew?"

I shook my head. "I nearly lost the best thing that ever happened to me because of him. He's selfish and manipulative, and I should have seen it so many years ago."

She put her hand on mine. "He wasn't good enough for you, Rowan. There was something never quite right about him."

I laughed. "I think you're saying that because of the way I feel about him. You never had a problem when we hung out together as kids."

"He always put himself first, love. You were so caring and sweet, I don't think you could ever see it. Maybe he does love you as a friend, but at times it was hard to see that."

She leaned over and kissed me, leaving my coffee beside the bed. It's funny how people are honest with you after the heartbreak. If she'd said that to me earlier, I would have denied it. Now it was clear to me just who my best friend was.

I was about to marry him.

THIRTY-ONE

KYLE

I STOOD UNDER THE TREE, waiting for my girl to appear. Nervous and excited, I knew I'd feel better when I saw her. She had that calming affect on me.

When I went into her room this morning, it was to reassure myself more than anything else. Deep down, I was still terrified that somehow she would change her mind and go to him. I should have known she would never do that to me.

My friend Neil stood beside me as best man. We had gone through university together, and while we were not as close as we used to be, he was the closest friend I had. Except for Rowan.

She was my best friend, as well as everything else. The bond we had was unbreakable now, and there were no more ties to the past holding us back.

We had so much to look forward to together. We had talked about finding a house rather than staying in an apartment. Apartment living was no good if we were going to have children. Holy crap, children. The thought brought a smile to my face. I had never seen myself as the fatherly type, but now I had Rowan in my life, I looked forward to it.

Neil's daughter, Rebecca, came walking out, scattering petals as if there weren't enough all over the place. Then Rowan's elder sisters, Michelle and Lindsay. Finally, on the arm of her father, my bride appeared.

Her hair fell in soft curls down her back, instead of its normal straight appearance. Other than Charlie and Andrew's wedding, I couldn't remember seeing her in a dress, but she looked amazing today in a simple white gown with shoestring straps. I held my breath as she walked towards me, such a big smile on her face as she came up to hold my hand.

"Ready?" I whispered.

"Oh, yes." She grinned, squeezing my hand in hers as we turned to look at the celebrant.

I can't even remember most of the ceremony, it seemed to go so quickly. All I knew was that she was my wife, and I would love her for the rest of my life. That part was easy with Rowan.

We had a barbecue as a reception, right there, out the back of Rowan's parents' place. Neither of us wanted anything too formal, that wasn't us, and throughout the whole event, Rowan glowed with happiness.

Afterwards, we drove to a motel for the night. I'd booked the best room in the place. It overlooked the ocean, and she stood on the balcony, the breeze blowing her veil behind her. She had never looked so beautiful.

"Come here," I said, loosening my tie as I came up behind her. She turned, leaning against the rail, a big smile across her face.

"What are you doing, Mr Warner?" she asked as I drew closer. I kissed her, pulling her into my arms.

"Kissing my wife." I said.

"Your wife, huh?"

I laughed. "Come with me." I pulled her by the hand towards the bedroom, not wanting to waste a moment with her. She was all mine now, and I just wanted to love her.

Unzipping her dress, I pulled it down to the floor. She had all that sexy lingerie on, but I wanted her naked and under me. *My wife.*

"You didn't make it easy for me, did you?" I teased.

She grinned, that beautiful, shy smile at me. God, what that did to me ...

"I thought you'd be up for the challenge," she said, looking at me with that wide-eyed innocent look. I took a sharp breath in. She was really putting it on tonight.

"You are a temptress, I hope you know that."

I was sure she fluttered her eyelashes. This flirtatious, confident woman was worlds away from the quiet, shy girl I had met. I loved that her confidence came from our love, from knowing she was wanted. Just the thought of her being mine tonight and every other night made me as hard as a rock.

Rowan knew what hold she had over me. There was nothing I wouldn't do for her, and I knew she felt the same way. I'd meant it when I'd told her she was my everything.

She laughed, pushing me down to the bed as she slowly stripped off her clothes.

"You are so fucking hot," I murmured, reaching out to tweak a nipple as she bent to remove her panties. She feigned surprise, slapping my hand before breaking out into a grin.

"Cheeky, too. Did you want a spanking, Mrs Warner?"

Rowan laughed, moving over my lap and leaning to kiss me. "You know what I want, Mister."

I grabbed her by the waist, pulling her around so she fell backwards onto the bed. Laughing, I moved to kiss her, my tongue finding hers ready for combat as we fought for control.

"Little Miss Feisty," I murmured.

"You know it," she whispered.

"I love you, Rowan." Her smile softened at the words. I knew she liked to hear them, and I loved saying them.

"I love you too. Always."

"Get up onto the pillow. I'll join you in a minute."

A quizzical look crossed her face, and she pursed her lips before obviously thinking better than to ask what I was doing. She wriggled up the bed on her elbows, and looked at me. "Well, come on."

I removed my tie, holding it towards her menacingly. "If you misbehave, I've got something to keep you in check."

She covered her face with her hand, laughing, knowing I would never, ever hurt her.

I stood, unbuttoning my shirt, putting on a show as she had done for me. Rowan convulsed with laughter, wiping the tears from her eyes as I stripped for her.

Then, I went after her, face-down into her pussy where I tasted her, teased her with my tongue. Rowan wriggled, giggling before I felt her push towards me, a low moan escaping her lips. Going down on her was always a pleasure, but this was special. This was our first time making love as man and wife.

"Kyle," she gasped, as I ran my hands up her body, feeling her soft skin beneath my fingertips. "Kyle," she said again, raking my hair with her fingers, arching her back as I slid a finger into her.

"Just you wait," I said, looking up at her. "I'm not in any hurry."

She moaned as I slid a second finger in, gently moving them in and out, watching the expression on her face as she lost herself in the sensation. I rubbed her clit with my thumb, smiling as her eyes rolled back and her body bucked, building towards her climax.

"Come for me, Rowan. Just let it go, baby, whenever you're ready."

I strained to hear what she said, a mass of garbled words as my fingers did their work. All that time she'd felt unloved, unwanted, when she had so much to give. I would take all she had, and give her everything in return.

Relentless, I kept going, stroking her just the way she needed to be, knowing her body so well that I could feel when I had her.

"Rowan, look at me."

She struggled to keep her eyes open, grunting at the effort. Focusing my gaze on her face, I felt her body stiffen, and smiled as she let it go, moaning as the orgasm took hold of her body. I knew just when to pull my fingers away, when to put them to my lips to get one last taste.

I reached over her. I'd put a condom box on the bedside cabinet, and both of us needed what was to come next.

Rowan grabbed my hand, pulling it away.

"What are you doing? I'd thought you'd have had enough teasing."

"I want you inside me."

I looked at her, confused. "That's what I want too."

"No, just you."

I raised an eyebrow at that. "You want to have sex without protection?"

"This is our wedding night. Shut up and fuck me."

The words were so unlike her, I burst out laughing. She pouted, and I kissed her, moving my hand to stroke her breasts.

"Rowan, I know we're both clean, but aren't you afraid of getting pregnant?"

"I want to know what it feels like for us to be together with nothing between us. Just one night. For me?"

I'd never had sex without a condom, but then again, I'd never been married to the woman I loved more than anything before. Her warm, soft flesh beckoned, and the idea she'd planted was all consuming as I sat looking at her. I was going to spend the rest of my life with this woman; everything I was belonged to her. My cock throbbed thinking of just how good she would feel, and I nodded, giving in to her wish.

Moving between her legs, I paused at her entrance. "Are you sure about this? I really love this idea, but are you really sure?"

"Yes," she whispered, pulling me down to kiss as I pushed forward. She felt amazing, wet and warm as I buried myself inside her.

"Jesus, Rowan," I said, trailing kisses down her neck.

My wife.

She closed her eyes again, and I watched her face as I thrust into her. There was a look of blissful surrender there, and I grinned as I picked up the pace, leaning over to run my tongue over her nipples.

"Kyle," she whispered. She stroked my hair, gasping as I sucked hard on her nipple. Grazing it with my teeth, I let go, looking up at her.

"Feel good, baby?"

She nodded, running her hands down my back. My body tightened as I grew closer to coming. Her hips bucked against me, pulling me in deeper. As if I needed any invitation. She was mine.

ROWAN WAS SO BEAUTIFUL. She was sex on a stick, and she still had no idea. We had screwed incessantly since that first night together, and our wedding night was no different.

Now we were spooning, my body wrapped around hers. She pulled my hand over to her, holding our ring fingers together, our wedding rings glittering in solidarity. "You're all mine now," she said, laughing as I kissed her shoulder.

"Always was. Even when you only wanted to be friends."

"Only because I thought that was what you wanted. I'm so glad you wanted more."

I pulled my hand away, running it down her body and between her legs, where that swollen nub lay, waiting for me to stroke it. She loved it when I gently sucked on her clit, trying to hold in her climax as I tried harder to make her come.

Her hips bucked back towards me, her butt pressing against my erection, which felt like it was growing harder by the second. As unusual as her request had seemed, being inside her with nothing between us made me feel even closer to her.

"Are you holding out on me, Mrs Warner?" I whispered.

She groaned as if straining to keep it in. I gently sucked at her neck until I felt her let go, her folds becoming slick as she moaned her climax.

"I love that I get to spend the rest of my life doing this," I said, and she giggled, parting her legs to let me slide into her. She felt so good, arching her back to push against me, and I sucked on her neck, hard, knowing what it did to her. I moved my hand up to her breast, rubbing my thumb across her nipple, hearing her moan at the contact.

"Today's the start of the rest of our lives, Rowan. The two of us get to make our life together now. No interference." She squeezed her legs together, and I let go inside her, groaning at how good it felt.

She took hold of my hand again, squeezing it. "It's not just the two of us," she whispered.

I rolled her onto her back, taking a second to register what she meant. Rowan guided my hand down, smiling shyly as she ran it over her belly. "Rowan," I whispered. She lit up with that beautiful smile, the one that told me just how happy she was about it.

"Wow. I thought we would have time by ourselves before starting a family." The words were out before I even thought about it, and I instantly regretted them as her lips turned down into a frown.

I took a deep breath. "I guess it just means we have to find a house sooner rather than later. Apartment living is no good for a baby."

That smile crept back across her face and she pulled me down to kiss her.

"Rowan, I would love to have a baby with you."

"Really?" she asked in that tiny little voice.

"Really. Now, we should get some sleep. We've got a long drive tomorrow."

She nodded, rolling onto her side and nestling back against me. "I love you, Kyle," she said.

"Love you too, wifey."

I felt her shake with laughter, pulling my hand in to her stomach tight. My heart swelled with pride at the thought of my wife and child. Nothing could beat this feeling.

THIRTY-TWO

KYLE

WE HAD our big annual tradeshow coming up, and with it, work was crazy. I spent all day in some big hall setting up stands and displays for doctors and hospitals to come and see what we were selling. It was a good way to drum up new business, and Dad and I threw ourselves into it. A few times I checked my phone in case Rowan had sent me a text. We usually touched base with each other whether I was in the office or not, but the cell reception here was crap.

By the end of the day, I was exhausted, and looked forward to going home to my wife. She would have left work for home by now, and if I knew her I'd come home to dinner waiting for me. I'd really struck it lucky with Rowan.

I loved watching her evolve into this beautiful woman who knew she was sexy, even if she still blushed when showing me just how much. That was so hot.

She'd been so tired lately, the early weeks of pregnancy wearing her out. We hadn't told anyone our news yet, and it felt so special keeping it to ourselves. I have to admit this wasn't anything I had planned for; children had always been a distant thing I hadn't thought about. But, at night she would lie with her head on my lap while we watched television, and I would rub her belly, knowing my child grew in there. It brought us even closer together.

The apartment was dark when I opened the door, and I looked around, puzzled. Her car had been in her park under the building, but there was no immediate sign of her. Unless she had come home and gone straight to bed. That was entirely possible with how tired she'd been. My phone had gone crazy when I got back into cell reception, but I hadn't checked it, knowing I was close to home. Anything work related could wait, I just wanted to be home with my wife.

"Rowan?" I called out to an empty room.

Then I heard it; the moan from the bedroom that told me all I needed to know. Something had happened, and I cursed at myself for not looking at the phone.

I ran to the bedroom. It was dark, but I could see her lying on the bed, arms wrapped tight across her stomach. The sorrow of her sobbing was heartbreaking, and I knew it had to be the baby.

"Sweetheart," I said, drawing closer to the bed.

She sat up, and I bent to turn on the bedside lamp. Her eyes told the whole story, swollen and red from crying and sadder than I could handle. I never wanted to see her like this.

I sat beside her, and she flung her arms around my neck, holding on tight. "What's happened?" I asked, fearing I already knew the answer.

"I ... I lost the baby," she whispered, and let out a mournful howl as I closed my eyes, stroking her hair and rocking with her.

"I'm so sorry," I said. She rested her head on my shoulder, her warm tears soaking the shoulder of my shirt. It didn't matter. None of it mattered.

"Miriam and I tried calling you and your father all day."

"We had no cell reception. By the time I got it back, all I wanted was to be home with you. I'm sorry I wasn't here, Rowan. I wish to God that I had been."

"She took me to the doctor. He couldn't do anything. I just wanted you."

"Baby, I can't tell you how sorry I am for not being there. Are you in any pain?"

She sighed. "Not really. It was all over so quickly because it was so early. Miriam wanted to stay with me when she brought me home, but I made her go. I'm just glad you're home now."

"How about I cook us some dinner, and we curl up on the couch and watch a movie," I said, "like we used to do."

"Yes please," she whispered, in this tiny little voice. She just sounded so heartbroken, and I had no idea what else to do.

"Do you want to come with me tomorrow? I'll call Dad and clear it, but I'm sure he'll be fine. It'll be busy, but we can hang out together."

"I don't want to get in your way."

I pulled her arms from around my neck, holding her back to look at her. "You could never be in the way. I want you close to me. I know how much this meant to you."

"You wanted it too, right?"

"You know I did. We can try again as soon as you want."

Her face lit up, and I knew it had been the right thing to say. "I'd like that a lot. I was getting used to the idea of becoming a mother."

"I want to make you happy, Rowan. I'd give you anything, if I thought it would put a smile on your face."

Her brows furrowed. "As long as it makes you happy, too."

I kissed her nose. "Don't worry about me. I'm happy all the time. I get to come home to you."

She smiled the tiniest of smiles. This loss had hit her hard, and there was nothing I wanted more than to see her lit up with joy. It would take a while, but we would get there.

DAD HAD BOUGHT a van to fill up with the trade show samples, and I had the dubious pleasure of driving it. The monotony of the drive was relieved by Rowan's presence.

Dad had been only too happy for her to come with me. Apart from it helping to take her mind off things, he thought my wife being there might make us look more of a family business. He berated me in jest that I hadn't come up with the idea originally, being his head of marketing.

When we arrived, he gave Rowan a huge hug, telling her that he was happy to see her. She looked around at our surroundings. We were in a big shed, with tables everywhere for all the different vendors. Today would be boring for her, though she had brought her e-reader so she could sit in the corner and just be there. Being together was enough.

The morning passed slowly as the crowd built up. While it was a specialised event, there were plenty of medical surgeries around, and people had come from out of town looking for new deals and any free trials of products.

By lunchtime, my stomach grumbled, and I peered at her, smiling as I did so. She sat at the back of our stand, having placed two chairs seat-to-seat so she could put her feet up. She'd kicked off her shoes, making herself as comfortable as she could under the circumstances. Engrossed in her book, she didn't hear me as I drew closer, and she jumped as I put my hands on her bare feet.

"Hey," she said, smiling up at me.

"You hungry? I'll buy you a hot dog and chips."

"That sounds pretty amazing right now." She pulled her legs up, slipping on her slides that were on the floor beside her.

"There's some food vans outside. Real classy stuff."

Rowan grinned. "Sounds like it. Are you asking me out, Mr Warner?"

"It would appear so. Come on."

She stood, grabbing hold of my hand and swinging it as we walked out. Dad watched us leave, and I saw him shaking his head with a big grin on his face. Us being happy made him happy.

I bought us a hotdog each and some chips, smothered in sauce, and we found a spot beneath a tree to sit. There was a gentle breeze cooling the otherwise warm air, the sounds of birds keeping us company as we ate.

"I hope this isn't too boring for you."

"I'm enjoying my book." Rowan laughed. "This was a great idea, though. I like being able to spend the day with you."

"Well, I like that I can keep an eye on you." I reached out, wiping some sauce from her nose that had rubbed off the hotdog. She laughed, kissing my hand before I withdrew it.

"I also like that you're laughing."

"Yesterday was really hard. It still makes me want to cry when I think about it. But I have to be strong and think about the good things. Like us trying for another baby. I'll never forget, Kyle."

I took her hand in mine, squeezing it. "Neither will I. You'll be an amazing mother one day, Rowan."

She grinned, leaning over to kiss me. Behind her, I saw a familiar figure.

Damn it.

"Kyle? Is that you?" Great. My overly possessive ex, who used to freak if I so much as talked to another woman. Just who I needed to see.

Shit.

"Uh, yeah."

Rowan looked at me with an eyebrow raised at my tone. I must have sounded reluctant to talk to her, which was exactly how I felt.

"Hey, Amy," I said. A look of understanding passed over Rowan's face as she got why I was recoiling.

"It's been ages." She came close, gazing at Rowan with a look I knew only too well.

"Yeah, it has been. This is my wife, Rowan."

Her mouth formed an o as she showed surprise. I remembered our parting argument when she told me I would never find anyone who loved me as much as she did. Well I had, and then some.

"Wife?" She laughed nervously. "Congratulations."

"Thank you," said Rowan, moving around to position herself

between us. Inside I was dying with laughter, my amazing wife showing her possessiveness to a woman who had taken her own to extremes.

"How long have you been married?"

"Just over a month." Rowan took the lead again, and I stroked her back with my palm to show my support.

"Oh, how sweet. Still newlyweds."

"Always," I said, leaning forward to kiss Rowan on the cheek. She nestled back against me, nuzzling my cheek in return.

Amy's face couldn't have been more sour if she'd been sucking on a lemon. "How lovely. It's good to see you, Kyle. Are you here with your father?"

I nodded.

"Great. I'll make sure to swing by and say hi."

"I'm sure he'll be happy to see you." Nothing could be further from the truth.

She sashayed away, an extra swing in her step, and I shook my head at her weird behaviour.

"That's your ex?" Rowan asked, her eyes following Amy as she disappeared into the distance.

"Yep. So glad I traded up."

She smiled affectionately at me. "I love you, Kyle."

"Love you too. We should go and relieve Dad, let him take a break. Only a few hours to go and we can pack up and go home." I reached out, twirling a lock of her hair between my fingers. "I'm glad you came with me today, babe."

"I'm glad too."

"We did need someone to do the heavy lifting when we packed up, after all."

She gaped at me in mock horror, before laughing. "Here was I thinking you just wanted the pleasure of my company."

I laughed, before my face turned serious. "Of course I do. I would spend every minute with you if I could."

AT THE END of the day Dad and I packed up the stand. We made Rowan sit while we did all the lifting. I wasn't about to make my wife do any hard work after what she'd been through, despite my teasing.

"I thought maybe we could play hooky tomorrow," I said, "and spend the day at home together."

She grinned.

"Perhaps you should say that to her when you're not in front of the boss," said Dad. He laughed. "Enjoy a day off together, you two. I think you've earned it. Just drop the van back at some point."

I nodded. "Thanks, Dad."

Rowan climbed into the van. I turned to Dad. "I'll see you some time tomorrow."

"Take your time. Your wife needs you, Kyle. She's more important than anything else."

It was a quiet drive home, and the large front seat of the van came in handy as Rowan snuggled up as close as her seatbelt would permit.

"You okay?" I asked her, just wanting to get home and cuddle up in bed together. I hadn't realised quite how tired I was until we'd left.

"She's really pretty, isn't she?"

"Who?" It took a moment to click as to what she was talking about. "Amy?"

"Yes." There was that little voice again. I knew her so well now that I recognised she was upset about something, or that there was something she was worried about bringing up.

"I guess. Not as pretty as you."

She rubbed up against me, and I knew she was holding back.

"Rowan, if you are bothered by her, don't be. She's nuts. If I never see her again, I'm not worried."

She put her hand on my arm. "I know."

I slowed down as we pulled up to the house, turning into the driveway. Removing my seatbelt, I put my arms around her. "I love you."

"I know," she whispered.

"Wanna make out in Dad's van?"

She laughed loudly, and I stroked her face, tilting it towards me so I could kiss her. "I think we should go inside and order pizza. We can eat it in bed and watch some junky television show," she said.

I pouted.

"Oh, and make out." She grinned before pursing her lips for a kiss.

"Anything my wonderful wife wants."

I made sure to slip the old tongue in for effect.

THIRTY-THREE

KYLE

I THOUGHT we would have a few months to get over what had happened, get ready to move on, but Rowan was pregnant again in the first month.

Rowan's pregnancy was a thing of beauty, at first, at least. She had minimal morning sickness, and although she worried after the miscarriage that she would have problems, everything went smoothly.

I watched my wife develop curves where she'd never had them before. She was beautiful regardless, but I loved watching the changes in her as our baby grew.

Before she got too far along, we found a house. My apartment wasn't small, but it wasn't the best place for a baby to live. Dad had promised to help us out, and despite being resigned to maybe taking months to find something, Rowan found the perfect place pretty much straight away.

There were four bedrooms, a big garage and backyard. But the thing that really sold her was the apple tree in the middle of the back lawn. I think it reminded her of her own childhood. She was happy, and that was all that really mattered.

Her proudest moment was finishing the nursery, ready for the little girl we were having. Rowan had been the one who'd wanted to find out what we were having. I didn't care, but the thought of having a daughter as amazing as her mother kept an almost permanent grin on my face.

In the evenings, we would sit together on our couch, while Rowan knitted tiny booties and mittens. Life couldn't get any sweeter.

The first two trimesters were fantastic. Rowan bloomed, glowing with good health and happiness. After the first few months had passed and we were out of the danger zone, she relaxed into it. I'd never been so much in love with her.

Towards the end, Rowan began to struggle. All the energy seemed to drain out of her, and she often just wanted to sleep. Dad saw how tough it was, and told her to finish up at work early. Always stubborn, she pushed on, and despite her protests, I installed a couch in her office. It wasn't long before I found her in the middle of the afternoon, fast asleep.

Her feet were so swollen at the end of the day, and she would grumble while I made her sit with them up in the air. I kept her wanting for nothing, although it frustrated the hell out of her that she couldn't do more.

Finally, with escalating blood pressure in the last few weeks, the doctors told her to stop working and put her feet up. Her arms were so sore, and the knitting she'd loved in the early days now made her hands ache. She had pregnancy carpal tunnel, and some of the things she'd been working on for our baby now sat unfinished, her hands too painful to continue.

She had gone from this happy, glowing woman to cranky and miserable within a few weeks. I hated what this was doing to her. Worse yet were the new body issues she'd had. Always so sensitive about her thin frame, now she would rub her belly and complain about feeling fat. But then, she was swollen from retaining water and didn't look much like herself anymore.

When she woke up with blurry vision three weeks before the

baby was due, that was it. She was straight in to hospital where they could evaluate her for induction. As far as I was concerned, the sooner this baby was out of her the better. She was far enough along that it didn't matter, and all I wanted was for them both to be healthy. Right now, I was scared.

I paced the room, while Rowan watched me, bemused. "Shouldn't I be the one stressing out?"

"What?"

"Well, you're the one getting wound up. I'm the one sitting quietly here." She smiled.

"I just want them to make a decision. I want you and the baby to be safe."

She held out her hands for me to take. "Kyle, I'm in the best possible place to be taken care of. Come and sit down. Hopefully they'll decide to induce and we'll meet our little girl soon. I really don't think I'm going home without her."

I squeezed her hands, taking a deep breath. "You're right. You're always right."

Rowan laughed. "I don't know about that, but I do know that the only thing we can do is wait." Even at this point, she was somehow the more logical and calm of the two of us.

As if on cue there was a tap on the door, and the doctor came in, Rowan's chart in hand.

"We have the blood tests back, and they all point to pre-eclampsia. So, the next course of action is induction. Let's get that baby out and get you back to being healthy."

She smiled at us and Rowan leaned her head on my shoulder. "See? It'll all be over soon."

"Yes, oh wise one," I said, bending my head to rest on hers.

The whole procedure seemed pretty straightforward, but it still took time. I sat at Rowan's side, giving her sips of water, talking to her, and wiping her brow for hours. She was stronger than I'd ever seen her, braving every contraction with the determination I loved.

From the evening when they started, she went all through the night. I could see her struggle with the pain, and grit her teeth, determined to just get through it. I would have given anything to take the hurt in myself, to ease her burden, to give her peace for just a little while.

And right at the moment I thought she couldn't be any more brave, I had two girls to love and take care of as Rowan gave birth to our daughter.

Our daughter.

THIRTY-FOUR

KYLE

I WAS SO overwhelmed seeing her pain and joy at the birth of our child, all I wanted to do was take her in my arms and kiss her. It wasn't my turn, though. Our baby was placed on her chest, with warm towels to cover her up, and Rowan and I both fell in love.

She was beautiful, with big blue eyes and tufts of blonde hair. Somewhere deep down inside, I fought the thought that she wasn't mine, that somehow Andrew had fathered this child. Where had the blonde hair come from? The thought of that made me sick to my stomach, but I swallowed it as I kissed Rowan and this beautiful little newcomer to our lives.

Rowan was so affectionate. She stroked the baby's head while squeezing my hand, saying all the right things, like how much she loved both of us. How we were a family.

Were we? Was there something she hid from me? I knew I was her first, but had he squirmed his way back into her life behind my back? I didn't want to be suspicious, but I couldn't help it. He was like this insidious parasite, ready to latch on as soon as he had any opportunity.

"Kyle?" Rowan looked up at me with so much love in her eyes, I felt guilty for ever thinking that way. Today we had become parents. Holy crap, I was a dad. I don't think anyone ever thought I'd have kids, let alone be married and blissfully happy about it.

The nurses took us to a private room, where the three of us could spend time together to bond. Rowan was just amazing. I'd gone to ante-natal classes with her, but she was on a whole other level to me. She knew just how to hold the baby, and with some help, feed the baby. I watched as she rocked our daughter in her arms, instinctively knowing just what to do. In comparison I felt clumsy.

"You should hold her, Kyle. I'm sure she would love a cuddle with Daddy," she said, smiling at me.

Still unsure, I held my arms out and she passed the tiny bundle to me. Those big blue eyes looked up at me now, and I smiled as I studied the little face. She had a tiny button nose; it was just too hard to not fall in love with her.

She was so precious, so small and fragile, and she captured my heart. Just as her mother had.

Are you mine?

I felt so guilty even thinking that.

"She has your eyes," Rowan said.

"Don't all babies have blue eyes?"

She laughed. "I don't know if all do. But I think she is going to. Just like her daddy."

HER PARENTS ARRIVED LATER in the day, and I excused myself to get some fresh air. My mind kept going back to the blonde hair, just like Andrew's. She was a baby, though; maybe that was something she would grow out of. I didn't know, it was all so confusing.

I stopped to get a cold drink before finding a seat outside the hospital. I watched cars pull up to drop off patients, and parents leaving with their babies. It was a beautiful sunny day with just a hint of a breeze, and the fresh air was helping clear my head.

Surely Rowan would be honest with me if this baby wasn't my child. She'd spent her whole life wanting to be with him; if she'd had the opportunity then why did she marry me?

"Kyle." Rowan's dad came up behind me. "I figured I'd leave the ladies to talk and get some fresh air with you. Are you okay?"

I didn't know what to say. "I'll be fine. It's just been a long day, and we have so much to think about now."

He sat down on the bench beside me. "That little girl up there is very lucky that she has two parents who love each other as much as you and Rowan. I have to admit, when we first met, I wondered what a big city boy wanted with my girl. She's so sweet and naive at times. You're a good man, Kyle Warner. I couldn't ask for anyone better to love her."

I looked up at him, and he had this big grin on his face, as if he'd won the lottery.

"This is your first grandchild."

He nodded. "Sure is, from my youngest girl. How backwards is that?"

"That's really cool." I couldn't tell him what I'd been thinking. Everything seemed so screwed up. I looked back down at the juice bottle in my hand. I should grab one for Rowan on my way back.

"There's something bugging you. I could see it when I walked in that room. What's going on, Kyle. Are you two okay?"

"It's just stupid. I never thought our baby would be blonde. Maybe if she had married Andrew instead ..."

He nodded, slapping me on the back. "Do you know that when we had Rowan, she had all this fine, blonde hair? I was sure I had a cuckoo in my nest. She grew out of it, and so will that little girl up there."

I laughed. "Thanks. I really needed that."

"She's not the type to cheat, Kyle. No matter what happens. I've never seen her so miserable than when you two were apart. You don't have anything to worry about from Andrew Carmichael. Rowan wouldn't look twice at him now."

"I love her so much."

"I know you do, Son. When you two are together, it's written all over your face. That's why I trust you with her heart. I know you won't put her through more crap. Now, come on, let's go see this daughter of yours again."

We walked back up to the ward in silence, no more words needing to be said.

Rowan's mother stood in the hallway, baby in her arms, and a look on her face that I'd never forget. I ran to her, looking into the room as she did and seeing the medical staff surrounding Rowan's bed.

"What happened?"

She looked at me, tears on her cheeks, and I felt my stomach sink into my knees as she tried to find the words.

"We were just sitting talking, and Rowan said she felt funny. She had some type of fit. I called for help, and one of the nurses fetched a doctor. I came out here to get out of their way."

I walked through the door and the doctor looked up as I entered the room. He opened his mouth to say something.

"I'm her husband," I said, making my way to her side. Her eyes were closed and my heart skipped a beat looking at her, she looked as though she was sleeping quietly. "What's happened?"

"She's had a preeclamptic seizure. We'll monitor her and get her onto some medication to help prevent this happening again," the doctor said.

She looked so peaceful, and I felt like crap for leaving the room, especially over something so stupid. There was no way she would ever be with anyone else. Not my Rowan.

Her eyes flickered open, and she looked confused by the people around the bed. She squeezed my hand. "What's going on?"

"Rowan, you had a seizure. We'll be keeping a close eye on you, and giving you medication to prevent it from happening again. You'll be in hospital for a few more days at least, and when you do go home we'll organise a care plan for you." The doctor smiled at her. "You'll be well looked after, even though I know you must want to go home now."

"My baby," she said, trying to see where the baby was.

"Your mum has her; she was in the corridor when I came back in. She's safe, babe."

"I want to see her." She was struggling to push herself up, desperate to see our daughter.

I went out to the corridor, smiling at Rowan's mum. "She's had a preeclamptic seizure. She's fine now, but she wants to see the baby."

She held her out to me, and I took my precious little girl in my arms. She gazed at me with those big blue eyes—my eyes. As if she could ever be anyone's but mine.

"Hey you, let's go see your mum." I looked up at Rowan's parents. "Once that lot have cleared out, come back in. There's not much room in there right now."

Her mother breathed a sigh of relief, closing her eyes as Rowan's father put his hand on her shoulder. This whole thing must have been as terrifying for them as it was me.

I kissed the baby on her forehead. "Come on, princess."

Rowan lit up as I sat back down beside her. "There she is," she said. "She looks content in your arms."

"She's so new, Rowan. She'd be happy wherever she was."

"What are we going to call her?"

The doctor, midwife and nurse filed out, leaving us alone for just a moment.

"I don't know. We made that huge list." I nuzzled her nose with my own. This beautiful creature we had made.

"Look at you, Mr I'm So Staunch I'm Not Going To Fall Apart When I See My Child."

Her mum and dad rejoined us as the three of us cuddled together. This was just awesome.

THIRTY-FIVE

KYLE

LEAVING her in the hospital was hard. Her parents went to our place to settle in for a few days, while I stayed as late as I was allowed to. I had hoped that this would be the only night we'd be apart, but it seemed we'd have to wait a few days to be at home together.

I got home, ready to collapse into bed, and the house smelled of dinner. Rowan's mother had cooked, and was waiting to feed me. I loved being part of her family. My father was in the living room with Rowan's dad; they were laughing together like old friends, and I stood and watched them for a while before joining them.

"How's it going?" Dad asked. "How are Rowan and the baby?"

I grinned, pulling out my phone to show him pictures. He smiled, shaking his head at the screen. "She looks like a real mix of you both. I'm sure that's Rowan's nose and your eyes. Look at all that hair. She's beautiful, Kyle. Well done."

"You have to come and see her at the hospital. They won't be home for a few days, so go and see Rowan. I'll probably be there every waking moment anyway."

"That's why we need to keep you fed and looked after." Rowan's

mother came in with a huge plate of food, and I stuffed myself silly
while they all talked and fussed over the photos.

Rowan and I hadn't spent a night apart since our wedding. The
bed was so empty. I missed being curled up with her, her warm body
pressed against mine as we spooned all night.

I even missed her cold feet against my calves. I just missed her.

There was nothing more I wanted now than to grow old with
Rowan, surrounded by our children. I guess seeing the birth of your
child makes you sentimental in that way. That's what it did for me. I
had a cold bed, but a warm heart, filled with love for my wife and
child.

I couldn't wait for them to come home, to hold Rowan in my arms
at night again. My phone vibrated on the nightstand and I grinned as
I saw what Rowan had sent me.

It was a selfie of her cradling our baby with one arm, breast-
feeding her as she smiled for the camera. I didn't know if she was
showing off her newfound abilities or just letting me know they were
okay.

> Me: You are gorgeous. I love you.

I pressed send and waited for the reply. I'd have given anything to
be at the hospital with her, but I would just have to content myself
with going up in the morning.

> Rowan: Can you bring my laptop in
> tomorrow?

I shook my head with a laugh. She would get bored over the next
few days; I guess it made sense she wanted something to keep her
entertained. This separation would be as hard for her as it was for me,
though she had it worse. At least I got to sleep in our bed.

She had the baby with her, though. Damn it, we still needed to
work out what we were going to call her. She couldn't be 'baby' her
whole life.

Maybe that was why Rowan wanted her laptop. The list of names we made was on it. Maybe tomorrow we would name our little girl.

> Rowan: I love you too

. There was another text, and I tucked the phone beside me in bed as I nestled between the sheets.

ROWAN'S MOTHER had cooked breakfast in the morning, and I ate quickly. The number one thing on my mind was my wife and child, and the sooner I could be with them, the better.

"We're going to do some sightseeing today, give you two some space. We'll be up in the afternoon," she said.

I nodded. "Thanks. Rowan asked for her laptop. I think she wants to go over the list of baby names so we can give this girl her name."

"Naming children is so hard. We struggled with all of ours."

"Where did Rowan's name come from?"

She smiled. "From a book I was reading at the time. I liked it, and so did her father. We might have rethought it if we'd known the teasing she was going to get. That was upsetting."

"I'm sure it was. I like it; it really suits her."

I grabbed another piece of toast. "Now, I'm in the shower. Be back soon."

When I came back out, I heard her talking on the phone, telling someone what ward Rowan was in. I assumed a family member or friend was sending her flowers, and thought nothing more of it as I set off to see her.

I tucked her laptop bag under my arm as I left the car. Just the thought of being with my girls again made me warm inside. All I needed was them.

He sat beside the bed, and the atmosphere was so thick you could have cut it with a knife. Rowan sat, paying all the attention to the baby and very little to Andrew, who was talking about something. She very clearly wasn't listening, and I could see the irritation on his face that only increased when I walked in.

"Hey, babe," I said, placing the laptop bag on the table beside the bed. She looked up at me with that hazy, far-away look on her face. Blissful and serene.

I bent to kiss her, lingering on her lips before nuzzling her nose.

"Now I know who your mother was talking to," I said, looking at Andrew.

"I got to the hospital, and didn't know which ward Rowan was in," he replied stiffly. I wondered if he thought he could sneak in and out early to avoid me. Too late for that.

"He brought flowers and a present for the baby," Rowan said. She was completely focused on me now, and I didn't know if it was a concerted effort on her part, or if she was ignoring him.

"That was nice. Thank you, Andrew," I said, smiling at him. All I wanted to do was to take him out and punch him in the face, but that wasn't going to happen.

"Thanks for bringing my laptop in. I had an idea last night on how to solve the problem of not knowing what to name this one. I'll just write a little programme, add all the names into it, and we can randomly select one and see if it fits."

I laughed. "Trust you, smarty-pants. It's as good an idea as any." I looked down at the wrapped bundle in her arms. "Want to come to Daddy while Mummy is putting you through the computer?"

She rolled her eyes as she passed the baby to me. Andrew sat forgotten as she pulled the tray table around and started up her computer.

I stroked my little girl's face. "We might just have a name for you shortly, sweetheart. Wouldn't that be nice?"

Rowan grinned. "Cheeky. Won't take long. I'll just put all the names in and we'll draw one out."

I looked at Andrew. He had this sulky look on his face, left out of everything.

"I'm surprised to see you here," I asked.

He shrugged. "I know things haven't been good between us. I wanted to show Rowan that I care."

"You have great timing. Rowan and I have never been happier. Our little girl is amazing."

He glared at me. "I'm glad she's okay. Her mother said something happened."

"Nothing we can't work through. Just means I get to keep a real close eye on Rowan."

At that, Rowan looked up. "How close?" She had that gorgeous grin across her face, the one she'd worn almost non stop since our wedding day.

"Oh, very close, Mrs Warner." I leaned over to kiss her. Never in my life did I ever think I would feel so much love. All for my wife and for my daughter.

"Give me five, and maybe we'll have a name for our girl." She was so excited, and I stroked her face with the palm of my hand before settling down on the bed with my girl in my arms.

"So, how are you, Andrew?" I asked.

He shrugged. "Okay, I guess."

I wanted to ask if he'd replaced Charlie yet. After all that crap with him coming onto Rowan, I wondered if he would just move on. But asking him that might prove to be the wrong move, and I didn't want to stir things up too much. Turned out I didn't have to.

"So, have you got a girlfriend?" Rowan asked, not looking up from the screen.

"No." He looked at her expectantly, as if he were waiting for her to interact with him more. Instead she tapped away at her keyboard, smiling as she finished what she was working on.

"I should get going," Andrew said.

"Sure. Bye." Rowan said. It took everything for me to hold my laughter in. Rowan wasn't giving him an inch.

"Are you ready?" she asked me.

"Ready as I'll ever be."

Andrew stood, leaving with room with just a glance over his shoulder.

"That was a bit rude. He was here to see you." I teased.

She rolled her eyes. "I don't care what he does."

Rowan turned the screen so we could both see it, closing her eyes as she hit a key.

"What are you doing?"

"What does it say?" she asked.

I leaned over to get a closer look. "It says Mia."

She opened her eyes, that grin slowly appearing again. "What do you think?"

I looked down at our daughter. She gazed up at me with those big blue eyes and I took in her features, nodding as I kissed her forehead softly.

"I think you look a lot like a Mia."

She wriggled in my arms, and Rowan laughed. "Aww, she knows her name."

"Mia it is."

Rowan pushed the tray table out of the way, moving down the bed towards us. She leaned over to kiss me, and I even got to slip the tongue in for just a few seconds.

She laughed. "You are naughty, Mr Warner. I think we have a name for our daughter though."

"So do I."

She waved at the baby. "Hi, Mia."

Mia wriggled again. *I love my family so much.*

THIRTY-SIX

ROWAN

ANDREW CAME to see me in hospital twice. Both times Kyle arrived, and he would sit and glower at my husband while we fussed over our daughter. I don't know what he really wanted; we weren't exactly close after everything that had happened.

Maybe I should have told him to leave, I had told him I didn't want to see him again, but I my head had been in the clouds since Mia's birth. I was far more focused on her than anything to do with Andrew.

Mia blew me away. I felt as if my heart would explode every time I looked at her. What I felt for her was on a par with how I felt about Kyle. My love for them both was overwhelming at times.

I hated being stuck in hospital. Not being able to go home straight away often left me weepy as I struggled with wanting to be in my own bed with my husband. I knew Kyle was frustrated too.

They let me go after a few days with no sign of any seizures. I was still on medication, and Kyle would have to keep an eye on me for the next few weeks, just in case it happened again. The thought of that was terrifying.

Finally, I got home, and I'd never loved it so much. Everything had been prepared ahead of time, but Kyle even had flowers in vases in the living room to welcome me. He was so wonderful, and I felt so loved.

I settled in on the couch with Mia. She had already started putting on weight and growing, and I couldn't have been more proud. I was glad that Kyle was taking time off to stay home with us for a while. Since the whole seizure thing, I'd been so nervous about it happening again. I couldn't bear it if anything happened to Mia.

"I'm so glad to have you home. I've missed you so much," Kyle said, nuzzling my neck.

"I missed you too. So funny, seeing as we spent so much time together."

"Our bed wasn't the same without you." His eyes were so full of love, and I was so happy to be with him again.

When Mia fell asleep, I laid her gently in the bassinet beside the bed. I wanted her near us, at least to start with. She'd been sleeping in a crib next to me at the hospital, and I'd gotten used to her little snuffling noises and snorts in the night. Feeding her in the night would be easier with this proximity too, although I hoped she slept well between feeds.

"I need to set the alarm for four hours time," I said.

Kyle looked confused. "What for?"

"To feed Mia again."

"Doesn't she just feed when she's hungry? What if she's hungry before the four hours is up?"

"I just want to get her into a routine."

"Does she need it, or do you? Rowan, I'm not going to interfere with what you think is best, because you are her mother and feeding her, but I worry that this is going to put even more pressure on you when you have enough to deal with. You just gave birth, and I know being stuck in hospital, and the seizure, have caused you stress. I'd like to see you relax, at least for the first few weeks, and the pair of you find your way together."

He did have a point. He'd thrown chaos into my life, and the world hadn't ended.

"Okay."

"Right. So if you're tired, try to get some sleep and we'll see when Mia wakes up. If it's too long then we'll wake her, but I am more concerned right now with you getting enough rest."

I was exhausted, and I pulled my nightgown over my head, and slid between the sheets. Kyle stripped off and climbed into bed beside me, holding me in his arms, and kissing me softly.

"I love you so much, Rowan. You and Mia are the most special, most important people in the world to me. It's my job to take care of you and make sure you're both happy. I'm just so glad you're home with me."

I clung tight to him. "I'm glad I'm home too. I just got sick of the hospital. Couldn't wait to get back to you."

He kissed me again. "Let's get some rest."

Safe in his arms, I fell asleep. Through the first night my memories were vague as he was the one who got Mia out of the crib, placing her in my arms to feed her before he changed her nappy and cradled her while I went back to sleep.

"Daddy's girl," I murmured, before falling into a haze of dreams.

THIRTY-SEVEN

ROWAN

I AM SUCH AN IDIOT.

Here was I, with my beautiful baby and husband who loved me, and I had no idea why I was so miserable.

Kyle was brilliant. He took such good care of me, but I couldn't bring myself to tell him I struggled to hold Mia in the early days. I was terrified that I'd have another seizure, that something bad would happen to her. It took everything in me to pick her up at times, but thankfully he'd been there to do it for me.

In the midst of my adjustment to all this new chaos, Andrew kept contacting me. I ignored the emails and texts, not wanting anything to do with him. For whatever reason, I didn't tell Kyle. He was trying his best to make me happy when the problem wasn't him, and I didn't want to cause him any more stress.

Andrew claimed to miss me, to want my friendship if he couldn't have anything more. I couldn't think of anything I wanted less. Kyle was the one I loved, the one I gave my heart and my world to. I would never do anything to hurt him, not on purpose.

As the weeks passed, our life got back to as normal as it was going to be. We eased back into our sex life, and I could not have asked for a more loving, gentle partner than Kyle. He caressed my new curves, kissed my stomach where Mia had been, and we both enjoyed my newly developed cleavage. Something was still missing, though, not quite right.

The body image issues I had were different now. I'd grown up insecure about the way I looked; my freckles, and how skinny I was. Now I looked different, and I was terrified that Kyle would decide he didn't like me anymore. I knew he wouldn't do that, but it nagged away at me, even as we made love.

I couldn't stay like this, so started a routine, taking Mia to the park every day for a walk. I'd feed the ducks, sit in the sunshine, and talk to her. I told her stories of my life, how I met her father, how I loved both him and her so very much.

After the first week, everything seemed lighter. The fresh air and spending time just relaxing with my baby was helping. She slept better at night for probably the same reason. I felt alive for the first time in what felt like forever.

At the end of the week, Mia fell asleep early for the first time. I knew she would be awake in the night to feed, but it was nice to just cuddle on the couch with Kyle and forget everything for just a while.

"You are radiant," he said, nuzzling my neck. "Something is definitely agreeing with you."

I laughed. "I'm just tired all the time, and getting out of the house has helped. Mia is such an amazing baby; it's nice to enjoy being a mother instead of constantly feeling like I'm behind."

"Hey, I like your behind."

"You know what I mean."

Kyle kissed me gently on the lips. "I know what you mean, and I think you are incredible. You're a great mother, and a wonderful wife. I know it's been rough getting used to having a baby in the house, but we're getting there, Rowan. I'm always here to help if you need it too. Don't ever feel like you have to do everything yourself."

"I know. You're so good to me. Things have changed so much, but you're always there when I need you. I've just felt like I've been in a bit of a fog lately, but I think I'm coming out the other side now."

He moved his hand to my chest, fondling my breast and rubbing my nipple as it hardened. "You like that, don't you?" I asked, laughing.

"You know I always loved your breasts, there's just a little more to grope now."

"What are you going to do if they disappear when I stop breast-feeding?"

He grinned. "Rowan, I don't care. You are beautiful, and I want to touch you no matter what. Sometimes the thought of you drives me to distraction at work, and I just want to race home and take you to bed."

"Why don't you?" I whispered.

"I thought you were trying to establish a routine with Mia during the day."

"I wouldn't object to an interruption from you. You just have to time it right."

Kyle laughed. "Tell me when her nap times are then, and I am so there."

"Let's go to bed now, while she's asleep."

"You don't have to ask me twice."

I laughed, getting up to walk to the bedroom. On the coffee table, my phone buzzed with a text.

"Are you going to check that?" Kyle asked.

"It's not as important as going to bed with my husband, whatever it is."

He picked up my phone as he walked past. "Are you sure? It could be your mum."

I rolled my eyes. "Fine. Whatever. I'll look at it, just get your butt into that bedroom."

He handed me the phone and I went into the messages. I closed my eyes at what I saw, before smiling. "Nothing important, let's go to bed."

"What was it? You looked weirded out."

"I'm fine."

"Rowan," he said, taking the phone from my hand and looking for himself.

He just stood there, looking at the screen. All the joy had gone from his face, and I would have given anything to know what he was thinking at that moment.

"How long?"

"I've been ignoring them, Kyle. I'm not interested in what he has to say."

"How long has this been going on?"

I shook my head. "There's nothing going on. He's emailed and texted me to tell me he wants to be friends again. I've been ignoring him because I don't want anything to do with him. I just want to get on with my life."

"So why didn't you tell me?" He looked up at me with eyes so pained it nearly broke my heart.

"I didn't want to upset you. I swear I didn't reply to any of them, Kyle. If you scroll through, you'll see no replies. You can check my email, too, if you want."

"You kept it from me, Rowan. I'm here to protect you, and you're keeping secrets from me."

I shrugged. "I didn't think it was worth mentioning. He's not my life anymore. You are."

He sat back down on the couch. All enthusiasm for what we had been about to do gone in a single moment.

"I'll tell him to leave me alone. You know I've already told him I don't want his friendship."

"This text just says he misses you and loves you. Do you know what this looks like right now?"

I nodded. "I know. But I swear to you, Kyle, the only man I love is you. The only man I've ever slept with is you. I wouldn't let him touch me in a million years. When he couldn't get what he wanted, he called me names and put me down. You would never do that. All these years I thought I was ugly and you made me feel beautiful. No one else ever did that for me."

He put the phone back on the table. "You are beautiful. He knows that, and he made you feel that way all of those years knowing if you had low self-esteem he would always have you as a back up. You do know that, don't you?" His eyes were pleading with me, his fists bunched, and I knew he was fighting the temptation to find Andrew and punch him.

"I do. I should have told you, I know that. You are just so perfect; warm and loving and sexy, and you love me and only me. I didn't want to upset you."

Kyle stood, taking my hands in his as he looked into my eyes. "There is nothing you can't tell me. This doesn't work if we're not both open and honest with each other, Rowan. What I feel for you is overwhelming, and the thought of you keeping secrets from me kills me. Especially for him."

I sighed. "I didn't do it for him, I did it for you. I'm sorry. The last few weeks, I've just felt so under pressure. I'm terrified after what happened in the hospital. To be honest I've been distracted by wanting to protect our daughter from anything that might happen to me, I didn't even think about Andrew getting in contact."

"What are you talking about?"

"I was so scared of having another seizure. What if it happened when I was holding her? What if I hurt her?" I could feel the tears building as the stress I'd felt finally released.

"Oh, baby. I could have stayed home with you if I knew you were concerned. Dad would understand. Nothing is more important than you and Mia. I'll deal with Andrew. Let's go to bed and forget all of this until tomorrow. Deal?"

I nodded. "Yes please," I whispered.

He smiled. "Rowan, you don't ever have to keep anything from me. I'll always be on your side."

The tears were coming now, and I struggled to breathe through them. Kyle wrapped his arms around me, holding me tight. "Come on, baby. I want to kiss every last inch of that gorgeous body of yours before we go to sleep."

He let go, holding out his hand for me to take and leading me to the bedroom where we could snuggle. I stripped off, slipping in to bed beside him.

"You don't have any idea just how beautiful you are, do you?" he said, as he stroked my breasts.

"You say that all the time."

"Because I mean it. Rowan, your body drove me crazy before Mia, and it drives me crazy now. Because it's you. I love you, no matter what you look like. Nothing will ever change that."

Tears welled up in my eyes, and I kissed him. "You and Mia are my whole world. Please tell me you know that."

"I do. Please don't hold anything back from now on. It kills me that you didn't think you could talk to me about any of this. We're supposed to be in this together."

"I'm sorry." I clung to him. The thought of screwing things up and losing him was unbearable.

"There is nothing to be sorry about. Just tell me that when you need me, you'll let me know. Don't be afraid to tell me anything."

THIRTY-EIGHT

KYLE

I LOVE MY WIFE.

She is my life, my whole world, the air that I breathe. No matter how much of a cliché that sounded, every word was true. She was from the moment she walked into that bedroom, the first night we spent together.

I watched her as she slept. It was hard not to, when she was sharing my pillow. We both used to be the kind of people that liked their space when they sleep. Now we end up on one side of the bed each night, entangled in each other as we dream together.

I had delivered on my promise. She needed to know how much I loved her after all that crap with Andrew and the text messages. It would have been easy to be angry with her for withholding the truth from me, but I knew why she did it. She was scared.

Her whole life she had loved a man who didn't love her. Now she had me, and she was terrified of losing what she had. But nothing would ever stop me loving her.

We had gone to bed, and I had kissed her beautiful body, praising the changes that she was insecure about. She got that look on her face that I loved as she came close to coming. That look of complete and total bliss.

Only I had ever given her that look. No one else ever would.

Now, she slept peacefully, sharing my pillow, her arm draped over me as she claimed me as her own. I was completely and utterly hers.

Any anger I had was directed at Andrew for targeting a woman who had recently given birth, who he knew was insecure about her body. He knew exactly what he was doing harassing her, and I was proud of Rowan for ignoring it. I didn't have to check her messages or emails. Her word was good enough for me.

She was amazing. Her whole world of regimented routine had been thrown out the window by a squawking tiny human whose wants and needs knew no bounds. At four months old, Mia owned both of us.

In the morning, I would call Dad, tell him I was going to take more time off to spend at home. He had been really supportive of us, and had asked me before if I'd wanted more time. As it was, I'd waited until she had the all clear from the doctor after her seizure. Now I'd found that even after that, it had weighed on her mind. That broke my heart.

My poor baby had been through so much these past few weeks, and I had been completely blind to it. I had been floating on cloud nine for weeks after becoming a father, and it stung to realise that I had been neglecting the one person who mattered more than anything.

Without her, everything else was meaningless. I slipped my arm out from under her, sliding out of bed and bending to kiss her cheek before going back to the living room. Picking up her phone, I read back through the text messages. He was begging, pleading with her to pay attention to him, trying to guilt trip her into seeing him.

As much as I knew she loved me, it surprised me that she hadn't bitten or given in. She was so forgiving and gentle that I was sure his grief must be weighing on her mind. Sometimes I saw her looking through old photos that included pictures of the three of them. Charlie's death still bothered her, and I understood that. For Andrew to play on that angered me beyond belief.

I looked back at the bedroom door. My whole life was in that room, and I'd be damned if I was going to let this continue. Tapping out a response, I sent a text back to Andrew.

> Me: There's a park near my place. We need to talk.

Seconds later, came the response.

> Andrew: I know the place. When?

Without even thinking, I felt my free hand form into a fist. It had been a fairly vague text, but he knew where I was talking about? Had he been watching her?

> Me: Ten o'clock tomorrow morning. See you by the duck pond.

> Andrew: Thank you, Rowan. You won't regret it.

Regret it? She wouldn't even know about it. My job was to protect her, and I would do whatever it took. Clearly her ignoring him wasn't bringing home the message. I would just reinforce it.

I smiled as I looked at her, still sleeping peacefully as I went back into the room. I slid in beside her, slipping my arm back under her neck. She stirred. "You're cold," she mumbled.

"You'll just have to warm me up," I whispered, holding her close. I closed my eyes, safe in the knowledge that she was mine, and always would be.

THE AIR WAS STILL chilly at ten the next morning, and I stood by the pond, rubbing my hands together to ward off the cold. I'd told Rowan I was going out to get milk, so I had to remember to do that before going home.

I saw him approaching, looking around for her. I'd pocketed her phone as I left the house, in case he sent her another text. Apart from talking to me, she barely used it and wouldn't miss it.

He reached into his pocket, pulling out his phone before seeing me. An uncertain look crossed his face as he stood staring at me, and I smiled back at him.

"Hey, Andrew." I waved at him, moving closer as he just stood there. As if he was waiting for something. The colour had drained from his face.

"Oh, Kyle. Hi," he said, looking at his phone and frowning.

"If you're looking for Rowan, she's not coming. I sent you the text."

His face fell, though I suspected he'd guessed that once he saw me.

"You have to leave her alone. She's not responded because she's moved on with her life, and she has no idea if you can fit into that."

He glared at me. "You don't speak for her."

"You know her well enough to know she can't handle confrontation. She has enough to deal with right now without the extra pressure of you wanting to renew your friendship. Personally, I think that friendship was toxic for a lot of reasons—mostly the way you knew how much she cared about you, and yet you did nothing to let her know that she should move on with her life."

Andrew drew himself up to his full height, eyeballing me and saying nothing.

"I've got nothing against you, believe me. And if Rowan wanted you in her life, I can't say I'd be happy about it, but I'd tolerate it for her sake. What I want is for you to leave her alone. If she wants your friendship, Andrew, she'll contact you."

He shook his head. "I should have known you'd stand in the way."

"I'm not. I only found out about all the texts and emails last night. Rowan didn't want to upset me. She's still dealing with the issues surrounding Mia's birth, Andrew. The seizure scared the hell out of her, more than she could admit. I'm looking out for my wife and her health, physical and mental."

As much as I just wanted to hit him and get it out of the way, there was no malice meant in my words. He was in pain from his loss, I could see that. Even if I'd seen him out and about drinking with other women, his loss of Charlie was as painful to him as if I'd lost Rowan. I had to admit to a certain amount of empathy. Losing someone so close must have been hard.

He shrugged, turning away. That was the moment I wanted to hit him. His complete lack of care for what Rowan was going through. No matter what, it was all about Andrew.

I watched as he disappeared amongst the trees without another word. I'd been more than reasonable; any more crap from him and I would take a legal course of action if I had to. I would just have to make sure Rowan was ready for that.

THIRTY-NINE

KYLE

ANDREW'S CAR was parked outside the house when I got home. I recognised it from the hospital, as I'd made sure he'd left the grounds before I did.

The garage door was open, and I drove straight in, running into the house when I heard raised voices coming from inside. I could hear Rowan yelling which was so unlike her.

Rowan stood in the living room, shaking as she stood looking at Andrew, her hands fisted up as if ready to protect herself.

"What the hell is going on?" I stormed into the room. She moved behind me, looking for protection as Andrew tried to reach for her.

"I put the bin out and left the garage door open for you, and Andrew let himself in. He wants me to go away with him, but I've told him that's not going to happen, Kyle. I swear."

I turned to her, cupping her face and kissing her. "It's okay, sweetheart. I believe you." Turning back to face Andrew, I shook my head. "You need to leave. Now."

His face distorted as a mess of emotion crossed his face, and I realised something wasn't quite right.

"Get out of our house, Andrew."

I didn't see him pick up the vase at first from the table beside the couch, but I sure as hell felt it as it slammed into the side of my face. My head spun at the sudden impact. The vase was solid glass, and didn't shatter but hit with a thud.

Rowan screamed, and I felt myself falling as everything turned to black.

MIA'S CRYING.

My head was spinning, my eyes blurry as I opened them.

Rowan will get her.

I shook my head, trying to stop the room from moving.

Rowan? Shit. Where is she?

Fear engulfed me as I stood, and realised someone was thumping at the door. Mia needed me, and I stumbled into her room, rubbing the side of my face, tender to the touch. No doubt there was one massive bruise where I was hit.

Mia looked up at me with those big blue eyes. Her hair had started to darken, and she looked more and more like me every day. Her little face screwed up as she squawked about whatever was upsetting her.

I picked her up and headed for the front door. Rowan was nowhere to be seen, and an ache engulfed my stomach at the realisation that she was gone. She wouldn't leave me, and she wouldn't just leave Mia; nothing would separate them. Andrew had to be responsible.

My heart raced as I ran to the door, finding two cops knocking. The female one recoiled at seeing my face. Mia had calmed, but still let out the odd wail to remind me she was there.

"Mr Warner? We had a report from one of your neighbours that your wife was taken forcibly into a car. I can see something's happened. Can we come in?"

"Oh God, he took her? Please." I rocked Mia in my arms. She

screeched in my ear, presumably annoyed I wasn't doing something to sort out her problem. "I need to sort my daughter out."

They both nodded, following me into the house. I grabbed a clean nappy from the pile, and sat on the floor. As hard as it was not to run out and try to find Rowan myself, Mia had to come first right now.

"You need to find her," I said

"Mr Warner, the licence plate has been called in and there is more help on the way. Can you give us any details as to what happened?"

"I came home to find my wife arguing with Andrew. That's Andrew Carmichael. He's been hassling her lately, and I told him to back off. Please, you have to find her."

"We will." The female officer nodded, still looking over my bruising.

"He was trying to talk Rowan into going with him, and she'd refused. I told him to leave and he smacked me with something heavy. Next thing I know, Mia's crying and you two are on my doorstep."

Mia lit up as soon as I put the clean nappy on her, and I hugged her tight. At least it was an easy fix this time.

"Do you have any idea where he might have taken her?"

Exasperated, I shook my head. "I don't know? His place, maybe. I don't know him that well, he was Rowan's old friend."

"I'll call a doctor in, get that face of yours seen to as well. Looks nasty," she said. I was barely paying attention to them; my thoughts with Rowan and my daughter. I hugged Mia so tight she squealed in protest.

I pointed at the vase on the floor. Made of thick glass, it had been the perfect weapon in the perfect spot for Andrew to hit me with.

"I'm guessing that's what he hit me with."

"Do you know why he might have done something like this?"

"Andrew's wife died on their honeymoon a while ago. They were both good friends with my wife, and he tried to turn to her when it all happened. He told her he loved her and wanted to be with her, as if she could just replace Charlie. The whole thing screwed him up. I told him to back off and leave her alone, and I thought he got the message. Clearly not."

They were both frantically taking notes. "The wife's death. Was it suspicious at all?"

I shook my head. "As much as I dislike Andrew, that's barking up the wrong tree. Rowan said Charlie had really bad asthma as a child. She had a massive asthma attack and it took too long to get her to the hospital. It's his reaction to it that's not right."

They sat, talking quietly while I looked at Mia. I didn't care what they had to say, as long as they found Rowan. Neither of us could cope without her for long, and she needed to be home, where she belonged. The one consolation I had was that Andrew wouldn't hurt her. Not if she meant this much to him.

"Mr Warner?" I looked up, and one of them was smiling at me.

"What?"

"We're going to set up base here, just in case you get a ransom call. There'll be someone on site to monitor the situation, but from what you've told us we need to find where they are and assess the situation. Do you have anyone who can come and sit with you?"

Mia gurgled. She'd be hungry soon, and I knew Rowan had some milk she'd expressed in the freezer. I should make a move and get that heated, ready for her feed.

"Mr Warner?" The female police officer was talking to me and I could barely hear what she was saying.

You have to snap out of it and pay attention.

"Um, yeah, my dad. I'll call him."

"I think you have enough on your plate. Give me his number and I'll call him. That little one looks like she's hungry, from the way she's pulling faces. Go and sort her out." I gave her Dad's number, feeling guilty about not calling him myself, but Mia was more important, and she let out a wail as I walked into the kitchen with her.

"Oh, sweetie, Daddy's got you." I wasn't as skilled as Rowan at doing things one-handed, but I found some milk in the fridge and heated some water to sit the bottle in. Mia fussed, and I clucked at her, trying to appease her, but I knew she'd feel the loss of her mother even if she wasn't old enough to know what was going on.

I opened the freezer door. Stacked neatly was enough milk to last us maybe the next twenty four hours. Rowan had to be back before then. *Please let her be back soon.*

"Oh, Mia." I sighed, hugging her tight. She started to cry as I tested the milk to make sure the temperature was okay, and finally settled as she started to feed. "I miss her too," I whispered. "The police will find Andrew and get her back, I promise."

I walked back into the living room. "Your father is on his way. Just let us know if there's anything else we can help with," the police officer said.

I nodded, barely hearing her. They needed to find Rowan as quickly as possible. For Mia, and for me.

FORTY

KYLE

MY MOTHER DIED from breast cancer when I was six, and Dad became everything. I still remember climbing into his bed and snuggling up to him, missing her warmth and her love. He struggled, but we got through it somehow. The sacrifices he made turned me into the man I was today. I knew I didn't always get things right, but I also knew that he was sometimes disappointed in me.

He was proud of me now, married to an amazing woman, and with a beautiful child. Now, I needed him, and he was on my doorstep, taking care of me again. The police still sat in my living room, waiting for a ransom call. The call I didn't expect to get. Andrew didn't want a ransom; he wanted Rowan.

For two days, stories about my missing wife were blasted over television and radio. A crowd gathered outside my house, a mix of supportive neighbours, nosey outsiders, and the media. Not one of them knew what I was going through. I'd had no sleep in all that time, and in the midst of it all, cared for our daughter, who pined for her mother.

It was some crazy hour, and Mia had just fallen asleep in my arms. I'd fed her until she'd fallen asleep, with that blissful full tummy look. Dad had gone out to get formula to cover the shortfall, the thought of that making me grimace. Rowan was so happy to have the breastfeeding relationship with Mia. If it were broken, she would be devastated. Mia had fussed at first, but hungry, she'd given in. Rowan's health weighed heavily on my mind. I had no doubt that Andrew would take care of her, wherever they were, but her separation from Mia could cause her issues. Whether Andrew was in any state of mind to realise that, I didn't know. All I did know was that if he laid a hand on her, I would kill him.

I'd called her parents to let them know what was going on. Her dad was angry, and I would not want to be Andrew if he ever had to face either of us. It broke my heart to hear her mother crying in the background. She was their baby.

Dad took Mia from my arms, smiling as he did so. She had long, curled, eyelashes that were just beautiful, and he kissed her little cheek before carrying her to the nursery. I flopped on the couch, burying my head in my hands. The police had an APB out for the car, but there hadn't been anything. Andrew's place was empty when they'd gotten there, and I drew a blank for anywhere else to look. They'd been to Rowan's old apartment to check, but nothing. This was frustrating beyond belief.

Dad came back and sat beside me on the couch. "Kyle, get some sleep," he said. "It's three in the morning, and I know you haven't slept since the day before yesterday."

I shook my head. "I can't. She's out there somewhere, Dad. I don't know if I'll sleep until she comes home to me." I broke down, and he held me while I cried. A cup of cocoa appeared from seemingly nowhere, and I looked up to see the policewoman holding it out for me.

"Tell me if you need anything," she said, smiling as I took the cup from her. I sat back, cradling the mug in my hands and sipped at the drink.

"Thank you." I sniffed.

"They'll find her, son. Go and get some rest. I'll be here if anything happens, and I'll come and get you. What's important is that you rest up and be okay to look after Mia. She's important too."

"I know. I just don't know if I can sleep without Rowan."

He grinned. "I bet you as soon as your head hits that pillow, you fall asleep. Especially after that." He nodded at the cocoa.

"I know you're right." I sighed, taking another sip.

"Kyle, they'll find her. They have to. If I know Rowan, she's not going to be sitting idly by. She'll do what she can to get back to you. You know it."

I nodded. "I know." I picked up Mia's drained bottle. "Mia knows there's something up, too. She's so unsettled."

"Sleep while she's sleeping then. If she wakes up, I'll get her."

"Thanks, Dad."

I finished the cocoa, smiling at him. "I'll go and lie down."

He patted me on the back. "Everything will be okay, Kyle. I just know it."

I walked into the bedroom, so cold and lonely without Rowan. Turning down the cover, I sat on the bed, picking up the wedding photo from the bedside cabinet. We looked so happy and in love. This was my favourite photo of us; Rowan looked so shy and yet alluring in the picture. Her hand was held up to her face, covering her mouth as she laughed at something I'd said.

I'd have given anything to have her with me. Instead she was out there somewhere, scared and missing me and Mia.

I lay down in the bed, pulling her pillow towards me. Her scent still lingered, and I hugged it tightly.

I just want you home.

Dad was right. After the cocoa and the stress of the evening, my eyelids were heavy, and I fought sleep for a while before it overtook me.

Rowan.

I dreamed of her. The night she entered the spare room at her parents' place, dropping her nightgown to the floor. Making love to her for the first time, her cries of joy smothered by my kisses so her parents didn't find out. The look of ecstasy on her face when she came.

The way she laughed, acting shy even after we'd made love for the first time. Telling her off for putting her feet on the dashboard of the car as we drove home together. She'd poked her tongue at me, pointing out the beach where she'd spent time as a kid, the place where Andrew's family used to have a beach house.

Andrew's family had a beach house.

That was it.

I sat up, looking at the clock. I'd slept for twelve hours, and it was mid-afternoon. There were spots of light through the gaps in the curtains, and I thought of my girl somewhere out there with the light soon fading. Maybe now I had some idea of where she was, but I felt like I'd wasted so much time coming up with it.

"Dad," I said, stumbling from the bedroom. He was fast sleep, snoring on the couch. Mia was in the arms of a policewoman; they'd clearly had a change of shift in the night and this new one was engaged in conversation with my daughter. Mia frowned, before lighting up at the sight of me. This wasn't Mummy, but Daddy was here.

"She's lovely," the lady said, handing Mia over to me. "Your father fell asleep, and I didn't have the heart to wake him when she cried. I've changed her nappy and made her up a bottle of milk."

"You're a godsend," I said. "I had an idea about where Andrew has taken Rowan."

"Where?"

"Andrew's parents used to have a place along the coast. It makes sense. Maybe he's taken her somewhere familiar, somewhere quiet."

"Used to have?"

"Rowan said they went there when they were kids, but they'd sold it years ago. Andrew was pissed about it; they used to spend weekends in the summer there. It's just a hunch, but it's the only place I can think of. His parents might not have even considered it."

She nodded, and while they called Andrew's parents, I picked up the phone to call Rowan's father. He picked up on the first ring, and I imagined him sitting there, just waiting.

"Kyle? Is there any news?" He didn't even say hello, and I knew he was as anxious as I was.

"No, but I had an idea. Rowan showed me a place a while ago where Andrew's parents used to have a holiday house on the beach. She said she spent summers there when she was growing up."

I could hear the excitement in his voice as he agreed it was a possibility.

"The police are getting directions now. If they can confirm it's the right place, want to meet there?"

The relief in his voice was obvious, tinged with caution as this was just a hunch. But I felt more optimistic than I had for two days. She had to be there.

I swung Mia around, to her delight, and she grinned at me with that gorgeous toothless smile. "Fingers crossed," I said, swinging Mia in my arms. I tickled her under the chin. "Maybe we'll see Mummy, sweetheart."

Both police officers nodded. "There's a helicopter being sent to check out the area. We should have some news soon," one of them said. I sighed, sitting back on the couch to wait for news.

I BURIED my head in my hands, waiting for any news. The police had requested a helicopter more than an hour before, and finally a phone ringing broke the silence in the living room. I looked up hopefully at the police officers, and the smiles on their faces gave it away before they said the words.

"Andrew's car is parked outside the house. Local police have arrived, and we've made contact with him and confirmed that Rowan is with him. He was agitated and hung the phone up, so they'll try again soon. We need to confirm that he has no weapons, and if he does, we need to talk him down before he does anything stupid."

The thought of that made my blood run cold. Clearly he was suffering some sort of breakdown, but he wouldn't hurt Rowan, would he? If he had in any way ...

"I have to go." I stood, looking around for my keys. All I wanted was to get in the car and get to Rowan.

Dad grabbed me, shaking me until I looked at him. "Kyle, you have to be practical. You can't do this without taking Mia. That little girl needs her mother, and Rowan will need Mia. I'll help you pack the baby things, but you need to prepare for the long haul if this takes a while to resolve."

I looked around the room again. Oh God, he thought there might be some type of siege situation.

"Uh, I guess you're right."

"I'll go grab the portable cot, and you grab the nappies and formula. Take some clothes for Rowan, too. She'll want them after a couple of days of this."

I rubbed my forehead. Of course he was right. The police were all over this situation, and with any luck, by the time I was there Rowan would be free, and I could hold her in my arms again. Just the thought made me dizzy.

"If you hadn't had that sleep, I'd offer to drive, but I think the fewer people there the better."

I nodded. "Her dad wants to meet me."

"Well, there you go. I'll be here just in case you need anything done back here."

He froze when I hugged him tight. Our relationship hadn't been a huggy one since I was a kid, but lately it seemed we were doing it a lot.

"Just bring our girl home, Kyle. She means a lot to me too."

I looked at him. His eyes were full of tears, and I knew he meant it.

I called Rowan's father before grabbing the washing basket and throwing it in the boot of the car.

It was probably mostly Mia's stuff, but there had to be some of Rowan's clothes, too. She didn't need that much to come home in.

Dad laughed, shaking his head at me as I climbed in the driver's seat and opened the garage door. The flash of lights from the group of media told me they were waiting for a story. They'd have to wait for a while longer. Dad waved as I backed out of the garage, closing the door after me. Like hell those vultures would get into my home. Some of them even had the nerve to chase me as I drove down the road.

I was glad for Mia's company along the way. It was tempting to speed, but with my daughter in the car, I behaved. She gurgled and grumped all the way, torn between the rumble of the car putting her to sleep, and being disturbed by her mother not being there. At least, that's what I put it down to. She was such an even-tempered child, but Rowan's sudden disappearance had rattled her.

"We'll get her back, kiddo," I whispered, as the car movement finally put her to sleep. So much like her mother.

I got to the road where I had to turn off, and in the darkness found Rowan's dad standing beside his car, not far from where he'd told me the house was. Alongside him was an ambulance and a couple of police cars. He hugged me, smiling at Mia, still fast asleep in the back. "How are you holding up?" he asked.

"Shit. I feel like crap that I didn't think of this earlier. I still don't know why I thought of it. Why here?"

He nodded. "I didn't think of it, Kyle, and yet I spent a lot of time here myself over the years with the family. I suspect he's brought her here because of all the memories. I spoke to his parents; he's cut himself off from speaking to them. They've been quite worried about him too. "

"Can we get closer to the house?"

He shook his head. "The cops said to stay back here, just in case he sees something and thinks he's threatened. They've called him to confirm she was there and safe. He was agitated, so they're giving him a bit more time before calling again, and are going to try to speak to her. He hasn't threatened her, but they're going to try to find out if he has any weapons."

I shivered at the thought of that. "Do you think he does?"

"I don't know. If his goal is to convince her to be with him, I can't see him hurting her. But, who knows what he might be thinking, the frame of mind he's in?" he said.

I nodded.

"Kyle, I'll stay here with Mia. You go down the road a bit and you'll find a small group by the side of the road. See if you can get more information. There are so many police here poised to get our girl out. We have to believe everything will be okay. They have the ambulance here, too, to make sure she's okay when she gets out. They seem to be confident. We need to be too."

I nodded again, struggling to smile. "I know. I'll stop being worried when she's in my arms again."

Moving away, I went down the road a bit, and soon found the group Rowan's dad was talking about. They were suiting up in bullet-proof vests, toting guns bigger than I'd ever been around.

"Jesus, I hope you don't think you're going to need those," I said to the really big guy standing in front of me.

He looked up. "Who are you?"

"My wife. He's got my wife in that house."

"Shit, mate. We're just waiting on word and we'll go in if we can and get her," he said, gruffly. He patted me on the shoulder. "I know this must seem scary, but we dress like this no matter what. We'll get her out."

Within minutes came the call, and he lit up with a big grin. "We're good to go. Sounds like the way is clear."

I closed my eyes, clasping my hands together. *Please be okay.*

When I opened my eyes, they were gone. Whoever thought big men with big boots could move so quietly? But they did. Now all I could do was wait.

FORTY-ONE

ROWAN

I KNOW THIS PLACE.

Some smells are etched in my memory, and it was as if I'd never been away. This house used to always smell this way after being shut up for the winter, damp and musty. No other place has ever smelled quite like it.

In the summer, we would come here every weekend and slowly the smell would lift, only to start all over again when the house was locked up for the winter.

Andrew had smashed the glass in the front door to get in. His parents hadn't owned this place for years, and we weren't meant to be here. I could only imagine that he'd chosen it for the nostalgia of the place.

So many summers we had run around on the beach, just down the road from the small house. We'd camped on the floor as there weren't enough beds, and before we got to our teenage years, the three of us used to put our mattresses together so we could talk when we were supposed to be sleeping.

This place brought back memories, but the mere fact we were here brought my anger bubbling to the surface. Andrew had hit Kyle so hard with that vase, he'd gone down with a thud, and I was terrified that he wasn't just knocked out. What if he'd really hurt him? Don't people die from blunt force trauma to the head? What if he was dead, and Mia was all alone?

The cold wind blew through the hole in the glass door. The panel wasn't completely gone, but it was enough for the place to feel icy. I shivered as I pondered the fate of my husband and daughter. Any good memory of this place was gone for good after what Andrew had done.

I'd fallen asleep in the car, despite my hands being bound. My dad always said it was the easiest way to get me to sleep, and I had slept through many journeys to this place. When Andrew shoved me in the back of the car, I'd tried to fight back, but he taped my hands together. I might have been almost as tall as him, but he was always bigger and stronger than me.

He tried to talk. I ignored him. Determined not to let him win, the only time I spoke was to ask to go to the bathroom. That was humiliating enough. He wouldn't remove the tape, and had to help unbutton my jeans so I could pee. The only thing Andrew was interested in was talking me into leaving Kyle and going away with him. Leaving my family behind.

I could see how time was shifting by the changing light in the room. Shadows shifted as the sun moved across the sky, and I tried to concentrate on that rather than him. Somehow, I had to get out of this.

Andrew's hand rested on my neck, and I couldn't help but cringe at the touch. In the past, it would have been so welcome, but now it was the last thing I wanted. He'd spent the best part of a day just talking at me about how we should be together. How Kyle couldn't love me as much as he did. How he'd always loved me. But nothing was going to turn my head or make me change my mind, because apart from the fact that I loved my husband more than anything, and I was terrified that he had been killed, Andrew made one very big mistake.

He'd left Mia behind.

My breasts ached from not feeding her, and while he was going on and on, all I could think about was how much she would be fretting without me. We were so tight, and I worried about there being enough frozen milk for Kyle to feed her, about how he would cope with her while I wasn't there. He was a hands-on father, but I was the one who took care of her most of the time.

She was only a baby, but she would know her mother wasn't around.

I wanted to hold her, smell her, touch my lips against her soft little cheek. The pain of being separated hit me again and again, and I feel a release of milk, leaving two growing wet spots on my shirt. He didn't even notice.

"Are you listening to me, Rowan?" he asked.

"Are you kidding me? I want to go home. I want my baby."

He sat down beside me. "Rowan, I need you to understand why I did this. I need you to understand why we should be together."

I glared at him. "You are crazy. My baby needs me, and you've done the worst thing imaginable to both of us. Go to hell, Andrew."

"I know you're upset, but I promise it'll get better."

"Fuck you," I screamed, and spat in his face. He stared at me, wiping his cheek with his hand. The tears were rolling down my cheeks at his inhumanity. He had wilfully separated me from my child, and I would never forgive him for that.

"Rowan, this isn't you. Can't you see how bad he is for you?"

"You know, all those years, I sat in the background, just hoping you would fall in love with me. I felt small, awkward. I hated the face and body I inhabited because I felt it wasn't good enough for you. Kyle makes me feel more beautiful than I ever felt possible. He's the one who made me feel, Andrew. The one who accepts me for who I am, and loves me for it. You never thought I was good enough for you."

He glared at me, his lips twisting into a snarl as I battered him with the words, the only weapons I currently had available.

"It's your fault that Charlie's dead. Did I tell you that? If it wasn't for you, she'd still be alive," he snapped.

Tears stung my eyes as I shook my head. "There is something very wrong with you if you think that."

"I told her, Row. I told her how I felt about you. On our wedding day, I saw you with that man, and all I could think about was that I'd made the wrong choice. It was all I could think about for days afterwards, so I told her."

"What the hell are you talking about?" I was screaming, my entire body shaking with rage and sorrow.

"She took off, and I went after her. She was so upset and she just ran until she couldn't anymore. I could see her, Rowan, I could see her struggling for breath, and I tried to save her. I tried to calm her down and called an ambulance, but it was just too late, and too much."

I tried to catch a breath between sobs. This was just so much to take in. "It's your fault; not mine. I loved Charlie. As envious as I was of her, I would never have wanted to hurt her. Why the hell did you say anything?"

"Because I wanted to be with you. You're so sweet, and gentle, and loving. Charlie was all those things too, but she just wasn't you. I realised far too late, and I'm so sorry for that. But we can be together now."

I shook my head. "The only reason you want that is because you realised I wasn't hanging around waiting for you anymore. I love Kyle, and Mia. Mia is my flesh and blood. You've torn me apart for the last time, Andrew. Kyle will come looking for me, and you are so screwed when he finds you."

He sighed. "All I want is to talk to you, makes sure you realise how much we need each other. It was always the three of us, Rowan. Now it's just us, and we need to stick together."

"Don't you understand that I could have been your friend? Now you've done this, you'll get nothing more from me. Not love, not friendship—nothing. I want Mia, I need her. She needs me. You've ruined everything."

"She could have killed you," he yelled at me, and I shrunk back away from him.

"What?"

"That fit you had. It was all because of that baby. I could have lost you because of her."

I could barely breathe. Now all his fucked-up reasoning was coming out. Charlie's death had pushed him over the edge to the point where I didn't even recognise him. All the years I'd loved him, I'd had no idea he was capable of any of this. I didn't know him at all.

"She's just an innocent child, I need to know she's okay ..." The heat of my rage was overwhelming. I didn't care what happened to him; he could go to hell now. "I was ill. It might have been because I was pregnant, but it wasn't Mia's fault."

"Relax. That baby is fine. I'm sure *he* is too." He rolled his eyes at me. Nausea washed over me at his nonchalance.

"How is she going to get food, Andrew? She needs her mother."

He looked at the floor, and I had no idea if I was getting through to him or not. Whatever happened, I had to find a way back to Mia. She was my concern. Kyle would be going out of his mind with worry too. I ached to be in his arms.

FORTY-TWO

ROWAN

DUSK WAS FALLING for the third time since we'd arrived, and my stomach rumbled with nothing to fill it all day. Andrew had given me water, but I don't think he had even thought about food.

"I need to go to the bathroom."

He sighed. "Okay, come on."

I stood with his help, and he led me to the bathroom where he unbuttoned my jeans, and left me to do the rest. I was glad that I'd only needed to pee so far, though that wasn't going to last forever, and I had no idea how I was going to deal with anything else. It was awkward, but I sat, wanting to sleep, but needing to stay awake. I wasn't about to give him the satisfaction of asking for help in any other way.

He buttoned my jeans again when I was finished, pulling the zip up that last little bit.

"This is embarrassing," I said.

"It's just temporary, until I know I can trust you."

"Andrew, this has to stop. You can't keep me here."

"I just need you to understand," he whispered.

"I understand that Charlie's death left you fucked up. It wasn't fair that she died, but you have to let me go. I'm not yours to keep." I sat back down on the couch, glaring at him.

A helicopter went over the house, and we both looked up in surprise. The only time anything like that was usually around was when they were policing the beach for someone lost in the water, which didn't happen often.

Andrew stood. "Do you think that's ..." He didn't finish his sentence as the phone on the table started ringing. He just left it, the sound echoing through the room.

"Nobody knows anyone is here, probably a wrong number."

It rang again. This time he picked up the phone, answering the call, presumably to get rid of whoever it was.

"Yes, she's here," he said calmly.

It's someone asking about me.

"We don't need any help, thanks. She's safe; we're fine."

"Help," I screamed, "help me."

He glared at me, hanging up the phone. It rang again and he picked it up, throwing it on the floor.

"What are you doing?," he asked. "We need more time to talk."

"I've done all the talking I want. I need to go home, Andrew. Please let me go home."

The phone was still ringing and I closed my eyes, imagining Kyle on the other end.

I love you. Please find me.

Andrew bent, picking up the phone and looking at it. "You need to talk to whoever that is, or they will just keep calling," I said.

He just let it ring and ring before putting it back on the table.

"We need to sort us out before anything else happens. They can wait."

"Andrew, there is no *us*. Not in that way. Let me go home."

He started to pace, clearly shaken by the call. Who had it been? At least whoever it was knew I was safe. Andrew had told them that much.

I tried to keep focus, but I was physically and mentally

exhausted. The only thing really keeping me awake was the constant ache of my body telling me to feed my baby. My baby, who was so far away from me.

I began to rock, trying to draw comfort from the thing that gave my daughter peace. At home, I would sit and do that with her for hours. She was such a sweet little thing, but sometimes she needed the reassurance of being rocked in her mother's arms. Now I tried to find the same comfort.

"What are you doing?" Andrew asked.

"I need Mia."

"Rowan, you need to listen, and understand what we have to do now. We can go away together, pretend that nothing ever happened and it's just us. The way it was at the start."

"That was a long time ago," I said, looking at him. He was slumped in a nearby chair, tired, and I guess, deflated that I hadn't given in.

"Do you remember all the fun we used to have at your parents' place? Playing among the trees? There was always somewhere to hide."

"Of course I do. It was also where I married Kyle. You know, my husband? The man I love, who I have a daughter with."

He frowned, placing his hands on his knees and rubbing, digging his fingernails into his skin as if he were trying to keep control.

"I told him to stay away from you, you know. He was never good enough for you."

I shook my head. I wasn't even going to engage with him now. My eyes were so heavy, and all I wanted to do was to lie down and go to sleep. His face was strained too, and I knew he must have been feeling something similar.

A few hours later, the phone rang again. By now it was dark outside, and the temperature was starting to drop. I could hear the weariness in Andrew's voice.

"I told you, she's fine. I guess you can talk to her. She's safe, you know."

He held the phone to my ear, and I nearly cried at the thought of Kyle being on the other end. Instead, a woman's voice came down the line.

"Rowan?"

"Yes," I whispered, trying desperately to contain the tears as I made contact with another human being.

"Just yes or no answers. Are you alright?"

"Yes."

"Does he have any weapons?"

I closed my eyes, knowing what was coming. "No."

"Hang in there."

The line went dead, and I started to cry at the thought of Mia, out there without me. I knew she had Kyle, but it was me she needed. My anger began to build again and my exhaustion amplified it.

"I hate you," I whispered. "I hate you, and I wish I'd never met you." Andrew recoiled as I spoke, each word hitting its target as my voice grew. "I loved you so much. More than anyone else in my life, I loved you. You threw it all away; you threw me away, and I'm glad you did, because I found true happiness when you let me go."

"Don't say that, Rowan. Please. I love you." He fell to his knees beside the couch.

"But you don't. Not in that way. It was only when you didn't have me hanging off your every word that you decided I was important to you. We were friends, Andrew. The best of friends. But, that was a long time ago and we both moved on, even if we didn't realise at first."

He was crying now, and for some perverse reason I wanted to comfort him. Old habit, I guessed. With my hands taped together, I could do nothing but watch as he broke down in front of me.

I closed my eyes as the door flew open, and heavy footsteps came past me. Shaking, I slowly opened them again, watching as Andrew was pulled to his feet and led out of the room. Surrounded by men clad in bulletproof vests and carrying guns, I began to sob as I realised I was safe.

One of them sat, pulling out a pen knife and cutting through the tape that held my wrists together. I took deep breaths to try to regain control. I didn't even know how long I'd been separated from Kyle and Mia. I'd be back with them soon.

"Rowan? Are you okay? Can you walk?" The policeman had kind eyes, and despite his scary appearance, I threw my arms around his neck and clung to him.

"You're free," he said. "Your husband is outside, just a short distance from the house, and there are paramedics to check you over."

I released my grip, leaning back. One of the others appeared with a bottle of water. "Here, you might need this."

"Thank you," I whispered. I took a big drink before standing, wobbling after sitting for so long.

Kyle.

It had been dark, but the area around the house looked like day with the huge beams of light from all the police vehicles. I took a deep breath of the fresh air before spotting him. It was over; this whole horrible thing was over.

In the distance, they were hustling Andrew into a police car, and he took one last look at me before disappearing.

"I'm sorry, Rowan." I heard him call before they drove away.

And then I ran.

FORTY-THREE

KYLE

SHE CAME RUNNING, stumbling out towards me. I ran, catching her as she fell, holding her just as tight as I could. Nothing compared to having her in my arms again.

"Hey," I said.

She gasped, trying to catch her breath as the tears fell, her relief clear for all to see. I had her back where she was safe. Scooping her up and into my arms, I started the walk towards the ambulance that was waiting.

The police car Andrew had ended up in drove past us. He could rot in hell for all I cared. The police would take care of him now.

My priority was Rowan. It was clear she'd been taken care of, but I was also acutely aware that not having fed Mia for several days, she was probably in a lot of pain and at risk of infection. Andrew wouldn't have had a clue about that.

"Where's Mia?" she whispered.

"Your father is with her. We're just going to a little spot down the driveway a bit and you'll see her. We have to get you looked at."

She nodded. "I couldn't do anything. I couldn't convince him I needed my baby."

"Does it hurt?"

She nodded again. "I feel like my boobs are about to explode."

I growled. "Selfish asshole. I hope he goes down for a long time for this."

Rowan buried her face in my chest, clinging tightly to me as I carried her the last few metres towards our child. Her father lit up as we approached, waving wildly.

"Is she okay?" he asked.

Rowan looked up. "I'm fine. I just need Mia."

He grinned, turning back to the car and lifting our baby girl from the back seat. Rowan wriggled to be free, and I set her down gently as she reached for Mia.

She closed her eyes, rocking the baby in her arms. "Oh my baby girl, you don't know how pleased I am to see you and your father."

"She's pleased to see you too. Little Miss Mia has been really scratchy without her mum. She knew something was wrong. Now at least we can all be settled. I had to give her formula for a few feeds, after we ran out of frozen milk. I hope you can forgive me."

Rowan glared at me, before breaking out into a relieved smile. "I know you had to do what you had to do. The sooner we can get back to normal, the better."

One of the paramedics was waving, and I pointed my wife towards them. Reuniting Rowan with Mia would probably solve any health issue she had.

She sat in the back of the ambulance, nursing our baby, and sighing with relief as they checked her over and declared her fit. She needed food, and we would have to keep an eye on her developing signs of infection, but at least now she was with Mia, they could find their own way back to their routine.

The local police wanted to talk to us, but understood we needed time to rest, so I found a motel nearby to stay. Rowan hadn't eaten in three days, and we were both exhausted. Her father stayed in the room next to us, needing to be near his girl and wanting to support us through this.

We ordered room service, but by the time we were halfway through eating, Rowan was struggling to keep her eyes open.

"Go and have a shower, sweetheart." Her father said.

Rowan shook her head. "As much as I want one, I want to make sure Mia is settled first."

While Rowan's father and I talked, Rowan snuggled into bed with Mia. The bottle feeding of the last few days had completely changed Mia's routine, but she fed from her mother enthusiastically and after what felt like hours, fell fast asleep.

"I'll clear out and leave you two to it." Rowan's Dad stood, and offered his hand for me to shake.

"Thanks for being here," I said.

I couldn't be anywhere else. I'm just glad our girl is safe." He patted me on the shoulder on his way to the door. "See you in the morning."

I went into the bedroom, and put up the portable cot beside the bed. Rowan tucked Mia in, standing over her to watch her sleep. Wrapping my arms around Rowan's waist, I looked over her shoulder. "She missed you so much. So did I."

"How did you know where I was?"

I shrugged. "I didn't, not for sure. I remembered you telling me Andrew had a place out here somewhere when we were on our road trip. It wasn't until the police confirmed that you were in there that I really knew."

She turned, cupping my face in her hands and pressing her nose to mine. Stroking my bruised face with her gentle touch, her eyes were so sad as she took in the damage. "I'm so sorry he did this to you."

"It's not your fault. Now at least the authorities can deal with him, and we can get on with our lives."

I felt her fingers run through the stubble on my chin. Shaving was the last thing I'd thought about the last few days, and I couldn't help but grin as I knew she hated it. Her skin was so sensitive that my whiskers rubbing against her would irritate it. I'd have to get rid of it before she let me really kiss her.

"I really need a shower. I don't suppose you brought any clean clothes with you?"

"Actually I grabbed the washing basket on the way out. Though, I have no idea what's in it. Hopefully it's not all Mia's clothes. You might have to go home naked if it is."

She wrapped her arms tight around my neck. "Just hold me for a second."

"I'll hold you for as long as you need."

"I haven't slept for so long, but I don't know if I can"

"I just want to cuddle up in bed, and I think sleep will come. Dad held the fort for a while at home while I had a sleep but I could do with just being with you." I kissed her again, and she sighed, her shoulders slumping as she relaxed in my arms.

"I don't suppose you brought a toothbrush, too? I'm sure kissing me isn't fun right now." She grinned and I kissed her again.

"It's not too bad, though I don't know if I'd use my tongue."

She laughed, and it was the most beautiful sound I'd heard in days. "If I shower, you can use your tongue elsewhere. It might just put me to sleep."

I gaped at her in mock offence. "Are you saying you want to use me?"

"Always." She slid her hands down my back, groping my butt and waggling her eyebrows.

"You always did know how to get what you want from me." I laughed, nuzzling her cheek. "In answer to your question, I didn't grab a toothbrush, but I notice that there are those kinds of things for sale at reception. I'll go and get you one while you shower. I need to grab a razor to take care of this."

She nodded, letting me go and turning towards the en suite. She squealed with delight as she entered the room. "There's a bathtub. I'm going to run a bath."

"You do that," I said, laughing.

It wasn't far to walk, but when I came back she was already immersed in the water, washing her hair with a little motel sample-sized shampoo.

"This feels amazing," she said, yawning. If her head hit the pillow, I was sure she'd be asleep.

"I bet it does."

"There's room for you here. Come and have a bath with me."

"You don't have to ask me twice." I grinned. "Straight after I shave this off."

I lathered up, shaving as I watched her from the mirror. She was exhausted, but the joy of simply being able to bathe was obvious. I frowned as she scrubbed her wrists, the tape leaving behind a sticky residue that was a pain in the butt to wash off.

Now, all we needed was time together. Nothing would ever make up for what Andrew had done, but being with each other was enough for now.

She wriggled forward while I stripped off, climbing into the tub behind her, and I settled back, my arms around her, my legs either side of her.

"Comfortable?" she asked.

"No, but I'm with you. That'll do." I pulled her closer, resting my chin on her shoulder as I stroked her thighs. "I missed you so much, Rowan. Never want to be without you again."

"I missed you too," she whispered.

"I don't know what happens to Andrew now."

She shrugged. "After what he did, I don't care. He tried to blame me for Charlie's death."

"What the hell?"

"He said he told Charlie that he loved me, that he wanted to be with me. She got upset, ran from him, had an asthma attack and died."

I sighed. "Rowan, even if it was true, it's not your fault."

"I know," she said, her voice dropped to barely above a whisper.

"He told me Mia nearly killed me because of the seizure. I was terrified he'd killed you with that vase."

I hugged her tight, knowing that tone in her voice, the one that told me she had tears in her eyes.

Planting a kiss on the nape of her neck, I held her until she turned her head to look at me. I leaned forward to look into her eyes.

"If anything had happened to you, I would have hurt him," I whispered.

"I know."

Her soft kisses reassured me, and I hoped my presence had the same effect on her. I ran my hand up her thigh, to her belly.

"Kyle," she whispered, and I lay back in the tub, tracing my fingers down from her navel to her clit. She gasped, and leaned back against me, tilting her hips to meet my hand.

"If you want to go and get some sleep, this can wait," I murmured.

"I just need you."

I kissed her shoulder and neck while picking up the pace with my fingers, stroking down either side of her clit. She guided my other hand to her breast, rubbing her nipple with the tips of my fingers.

In silence, we sat, with just the gentle sound of the water moving as I felt her body tense. She moaned, rubbing hard against my fingers as she found her release, reaching for my hand under the water and stroking the back of it.

"I love you," she whispered, raising my hand from the water and gripping it in hers.

"I love you too. More than anything."

"Let's go to bed."

Falling asleep was easy, my arms around her, feeling her soft body beside me, listening to her breathing get slower as she fell asleep. Despite the sleep I'd had at home, exhaustion overtook me.

She was safe.

FORTY-FOUR

ROWAN

MIA SLEPT for most of the night, stirring in the small hours just before the sunrise. Before I could react, Kyle sprang up, picking her up out of the cot, and changing her nappy before bringing her back to bed. I smiled as he cooed to calm her. Only a few months old, but she knew exactly who she belonged to as she let out a big grin for Daddy.

She yawned sleepily, and I nuzzled her face as he passed her to me, breathing in the milky, baby smell of my daughter. I never wanted to be away from her again.

"Hey," I heard Kyle whisper, slipping his arm around my waist. He sat beside me in the bed, his eyes filled with concern for the tears that had started inexplicably falling. I didn't know why I was crying, but with the release of the tears, anxiety flowed out of me. I was still so wound up over the events over the last few days, but I was so happy to be reunited with my family. Still, just a little part of me mourned for the friendship that would be forever lost.

Nothing would ever heal the wound in my heart from Charlie's death. Despite our differences, I had loved her for so long, and the thought of a world without her still tore me apart when I thought about it. Where Andrew was concerned, I felt numb, and I wondered what my life would have been without him in it.

Kyle kissed my cheek, wiping my tears with his thumb and pressing his nose to mine as I turned toward him. I laughed as Mia let out a hungry wail. "I'm sorry, sweetheart. I hadn't forgotten you." Lifting her to my breast, I closed my eyes as she fed, gulping the milk down as if it were the last feed she would ever have. I looked down at her, stroking her head with my fingers. Poor little mite, she probably thought it would be the last feed.

"Mummy's not going anywhere, again," I whispered, feeling Kyle's chin resting on my shoulder. I leaned my head towards him. Just the contact was enough to soothe my aching soul. Sitting here with Kyle and Mia, I felt safe and loved.

We watched the sun come up as Mia continued to feed, and my eyes were trying desperately to close as she drew closer to filling her stomach.

"Here," Kyle whispered, taking her in his arms. Her little eyes were already closed, and he kissed her forehead as he turned to place her back in the cot. "She's as exhausted from all this as we are."

"I can't wait to go home."

He climbed back into bed. "Neither can I."

"When are the police coming to talk to us again?"

"In a few hours. Get some more sleep, Rowan. I'll be right here."

I nodded, sinking into the softness of the pillows. My own bed would be preferable, but this one would do quite nicely right now. The world closed in around me as I sunk into the oblivion of sleep, safe in the knowledge my family was with me, and we would be okay.

I HAD NEVER BEEN SO glad to see our house in all my life. Kyle's dad was there to greet us, and he hugged me and Mia, welcoming us home.

Home. This place felt more like home than ever. I'd fallen in love when we'd found it, but now it meant so much more to me. This was where Kyle and I would raise our children. Mia would play with her siblings in the backyard, which wasn't like the orchard, but it was still perfection.

The events of the last few days felt distant now, even though it was only yesterday when the whole thing had ended. My earlier fierce loyalty to Andrew had dwindled to the point where I felt nothing. Separating me from Mia had been the last straw. Nothing mattered to me more than Kyle and Mia; there was simply no competition.

My only worry was going to court with Andrew. The thought of seeing him again turned my stomach, but then he confessed to everything and pleaded guilty, removing the need for me to see him. There would be jail time, though this was reduced in part by his lawyer bringing up the death of Charlie. Despite my disgust at him, I understood

Kyle was by my side through it all, never judging me when the memories of Charlie's death came to the surface and I cried for all three of us. He knew that Andrew spending time in prison saddened me, but also knew that my family came before anything else.

And then we got on with our lives.

EPILOGUE

Three years later

PREPARING dinner was so much easier when I didn't have a toddler running circles around me. Literally. There was nowhere I could move where Mia wasn't under my feet as she tried to play.

"How do you still have energy?" I asked, picking her up as she giggled, covering her mouth with her hand. We shared a lot of mannerisms, but she was a lot more outgoing than I had ever been, and was one of the popular kids at her day-care.

I'd gone back to work when she was one year old, part-time at first, and then full-time when Ross retired. Kyle's father had gradually given me more and more to do as his faith in Ross diminished. Realising his time was up, and with no chance of pushing me out of the way, he moved along. Now, I was the IT Manager, with an assistant of my own, and complete control of everything.

I worked the hours I wanted, which suited me down to the ground. Leaving mid-afternoon every day meant I could pick up Mia and spend time with her before Kyle came home. Other than Kyle, she was my world, so much like me and yet enough of her father that she wouldn't have to deal with the same taunts I did when I had been growing up.

"Daddy," she squealed in my ear, spotting Kyle before I did. She wriggled in my arms, and I dropped her to the floor so she could go running to him.

"Hey, princess," he said, opening his arms for her to jump into. He stroked her hair as she hugged him tight, and she let go just enough for him to give her a kiss.

"Hi, princess," he said again, coming to my side. I grinned as his lips lingered on mine, Mia giggling at the sight of us kissing.

Mia fell asleep at the dinner table, and Kyle tucked her into bed before joining me in the kitchen where I stood, loading the dishwasher. He patted me on the butt as I placed the dishes in the tray, and I stood up to kiss him. Pressing me against the bench, his tongue pushed at mine and he ran his hands down my back. All this time and we were still like newlyweds.

"Want to go to bed early?" I asked, when he finally let me go.

"We need to talk first." He looked serious, and I stroked his cheek with my palm, trying to get him to meet my eye.

"Kyle? What is it?"

He took my hand, leading me into the living room, and we sat on the couch hand in hand as he tried to come out with whatever it was he had to tell me. My stomach churned at the thought of what it could be. We were so blissfully happy, I couldn't think of anything.

"Andrew wants to see you."

I could feel the colour draining from my face as his words sunk in. That was one possibility I'd never considered.

"How do you know?"

"He called me. He knows he can't make contact with you, Rowan. That would get him into far too much trouble. Hell, I nearly hung up on him, but I wanted to make sure there was no more bullshit going on. I think he wants to apologise."

Kyle looked up at me, his blue eyes filled with concern. "Look, Rowan, whatever you decide I'll back you. I'm not letting you be alone with him, but if you want to give him the opportunity to say he's sorry, I'm not going to stand in the way."

For the first time in a long time, I just didn't know what to do. Part of me wanted to see him, hear what he had to say for himself and then send him on his way. But another part of me felt I'd turned my back on that part of my life, so immersed in my new life as I was.

"Let him say his piece," I croaked, "but I want you with me the whole time."

He nodded. "Okay, I'll call him tomorrow and give him your rules. He was very humble on the phone. I'm the last person to stick up for him, but we talked enough that I think he just wants to say he's sorry. I guess Charlie's death was a few years ago now; maybe he's put to rest some of the things that haunted him."

Kyle wrapped his harms around me, kissing my cheek. "Either way, I'm happy for you to make the decision to see him or not. Any time you want to change your mind, just let me know. You don't have to go through with this."

"I know. But I think it's best to get this over with, and then we can get on with our lives."

He ran his finger down my chest, between my breasts, and lingered at the top of my stomach. "I think we can make a start on that now. Let's go to bed and worry about it in the morning."

I grinned. "That sounds like the best offer I've had all day."

———

ANDREW SAT on the park bench, throwing bread at the ducks. This was the same place Kyle had told him to leave me alone, as I discovered after the fact. If only he'd listened, maybe we would have been able to salvage some kind of friendship. Now, that was impossible.

Kyle grabbed my arm as we approached. "Remember, Rowan. He's not supposed to get within a hundred metres of you. You don't have to be here."

I took a deep breath. "I know. I want to do this."

"I'll be right here watching. You just have to wave if you need help."

Wrapping my arms around his waist, I hugged him tightly. "I love you."

He kissed the top of my head, and I closed my eyes, just breathing him in. I let go, and looked at him. "I won't be long."

Andrew didn't even look up when I approached, and I sat just watching him throwing bread for a moment. He looked up when he ran out of bread, smiling, his eyes filled with sadness.

"Hey, Rowan. I'm glad you came to talk to me."

"I'm not here for long, and Kyle is right over there."

He shook his head. "I'm not going to try anything. We're way past that. I've had a lot of time to think about what I did, and I can't really believe that I did it."

"I get that you were a bit crazy over Charlie's death. I was devastated too, and you knew it. There's no excuse for what you did, Andrew."

He looked at the ground. "I know, and I'm so sorry. All I could think about was trying to get you to understand that we needed to be together, and yet, I knew you were far happier with Kyle than you ever would have been with me. The thought of leaving your baby behind just kills me now. You were so right; I didn't check that Kyle wasn't more badly injured, and just left without another thought. If anything had happened to her ..."

I could see the struggle he fought within himself as he relived those days. It was nothing I hadn't been through, and maybe I should have felt for him as he realised the extent of what he'd done. But I still felt nothing.

"How is she?" he asked. "How is your little girl?"

"She's amazing. Looks a lot like me, straight brown hair. No freckles, though. Well, maybe the odd one, but she's more like Kyle in that way. She's smart and pretty."

"Just like her mother." His blue eyes bored into me, his mouth upturned in a small smile.

"We've got another one on the way. Early days, but we're hopeful everything will go well." I looked down at the ducks, gradually coming closer and closer for bread. "I wish none of this had happened, Andrew. I could have just pictured yours and Charlie's children playing with mine. We all could have been happy."

He sighed. "I lied about what happened on our honeymoon. Charlie did get upset, but it didn't quite go the way I said. She noticed the way I reacted to Kyle at the wedding, and picked up that I had an issue with him. She loved you so much, she was worried that I might interfere with your relationship, push you further away. That's what we argued about. It was my problem, not yours. I wanted you to know"

I buried my head in my hands as the tears came, and when I looked up, Kyle was running towards me. I held up my hand to tell him to stop, and saw him come to a halt.

"I loved both of you," I whispered, "but Kyle's all mine. I don't share him with anyone but Mia, and that's different. Maybe I needed for you two to be together in order to find myself. I'm only sorry Charlie's not here to share this, for me to tell her just how full my life is now. All it took was for me to get over you."

I stood. This had been the last goodbye to my old life, and my husband waited for me as we started on the next part of the new.

Andrew looked up at me. He looked the way he did at Charlie's funeral, full of loss and remorse.

"Get better, Andrew. Find a way to move on and be happy. You deserve that."

"Love you, Rowan. Always have, always will," he said softly.

I turned, walking towards Kyle, and then running as the weight of the conversation lifted. Throwing myself at him, I flung my arms around his neck, and he spun me around, laughing before kissing me in that way only he could.

"You okay?" he whispered.

"I'll be fine. Let's go and pick up Mia from day-care. I think we all need to spend the rest of the day together."

He grinned. "Good thinking. You should put your feet up anyway. I'm sure today will be stressful enough without running around after the rest of us."

Kyle held my hand tight, the cold wind freezing the tears on my cheeks as we walked away without a glance behind.

Home was warm when we got there, though the chill was setting in outside. Mia rode her tricycle around the backyard, pushed across the grass by Kyle as I watched the two of them.

I smiled, looking at the apple tree in the middle of the yard. Blossoms had started to coat the branches, and brought with them the promise of warmer weather. It made me think of home, of the early days, of Andrew, and of Charlie, who didn't get to see the orchard in all its glory, and who never would.

"Goodbye, Charlie," I whispered.

Kyle looked up as I shivered, and shook his head at Mia. "We should go inside now, sweetheart. It's cold out here and not good for you, or your mother."

"Aww, Daddy," she whined.

He leaned over, tapping her on the nose. "Tell you what. If you come inside with me now, I'll make you a nice hot chocolate with marshmallows. I understand your mother is fond of them too."

Picking her up in one arm, the tricycle in the other, he brought them both to the back door, dropping the trike on the deck as he carried our daughter inside the house with me following behind.

I didn't need the hot chocolate to warm me. I had the love that I felt for the pair of them, and in the months to come, that love would grow just that little bit more.

Best of all, now and forever, no matter what else happened to us along the way, Kyle was my best friend.

And he always would be.

ALSO BY WENDY SMITH

Coming Home

Doctor's Orders

Baker's Dozen

Hunter's Mark

Teacher's Pet

A Very Campbell Christmas

Fall and Rise Duet

Falling

Rising

Fall and Rise - The Complete Duet

The Aeon Series

Game On

Build a Nerd

Bar None

Hollywood Kiwis Series

Common Ground

Even Ground

Under Ground

Rocky Ground

Coming soon Solid Ground

Stand alones

For the Love of Chloe

Only Ever You

The Friends Duet
Loving Rowan
Three Days

The Forever Series
Something Real
The Right One
Unexpected

Chances Series
Another Chance
Taking Chances

Lifetime Series
In a Lifetime
In an Instant
In a Heartbeat
In the End
At the Start